LONERS

THOMAS ROUSH

TABLE OF CONTENTS

FOREWORD

In our world of abundance, there is an ongoing struggle for meaning and purpose. This struggle affects men in unique ways. When survival was predicated on difficult daily effort, and the threats to survival were real and easily identified, men had no trouble finding their purpose. They struggled with meaning then as well, as documented in the literature of antiquity, but for the overwhelming majority, a man's daily tasks kept him occupied and supplied a sort of daily measuring stick of progress. The fields were brought in, the animal husbandry tasks were accomplished, and the women and children were defended. Only at night when he was accompanied by the stars, or perhaps when he was participating in a formal religious practice, did he think of the larger purpose of his toil.

With the arrival of industrialization and modernity, a man transferred his destiny from nature to society. In exchange for material abundance, all of humanity turned their fate over to each other, and the abstract forces of law and economics. This exchange displaced the moral order that preceded it. Men were cast into a world of far more complex roles and identities. Relationships that were stable for centuries suddenly had different rules and outcomes.

The late 19th century and early 20th century saw an unprecedented wave of invention and industrialization that is recorded in the art and music of the world. The classical period gave way to the modernist period in a way recorded by every form of human creativity, including literature. The displaced purpose of a man's life is captured repeatedly in the works of Ernest Hemingway. Hemingway was a masterful novelist and he was also an accomplished short story writer. His short stories feature a recurring character named Nick Adams that is a thinly veiled young Hemingway. Like Hemingway, Nick is injured in World War 1, and also like Hemingway, Nick struggles to stabilize and find satisfying relationships.

I've come back to the Hemingway character of Nick Adams at various times in my life and continually found him to be relevant. Our 21st-century world is no less displacing than that of the early 20th-century world inhabited by Hemingway's Nick Adams. In many critical ways, the displacement of men has become far more acute. Our culture allocates even less relevance to traditional manhood.

The Nick character contained in many of the stories presented here is an early 21st century contemporary of Hemingway's 20th-century version. Nick and the other men within this collection are struggling to find order in a world with plenty of everything except meaning. In the void, each searches for 'a separate peace.'

— Tom Roush

CHECK POINT

During the day, bright orange and white helicopters would practice landing in the giant field at the end of the road. Young Nick would walk to the end of the road and lean on the barbed wire fence and watch them. They would come in pairs now and again, but mostly, they came one at a time, landed, and then before their rotors had even slowed, they would take off again.

The large helos would land towards the middle of the field which was so large that Nick could hear the thumping of the rotors but barely see the pilots through the open side doors. They would come in low and fast, touch their skids down, and then the motors would rev up high, the skids would slowly lift off the ground, the entire craft would pitch forward, and be gone.

From the fathers of his friends, he learned that these were Navy and Marine training helos, and the entire field was controlled by the

Navy. The sound of Navy and Marine choppers thumping overhead was ubiquitous in his neighborhood. It was the background sound of war seen on TV.

One of Nick's friends had an older brother who was a mechanic on an aircraft carrier, and he provided a few precious details from the war the adults were talking about. The older brother was sitting in a folding lawn chair by the fence watching the helos come and go. He sipped from a can of beer.

"We spend a lot of time moving shit back and forth off them ships," he said to Nick and Nick's friend. "It's a long way from the ship to the shore. Vietnam's such a shithole they don't hardly have ports, so we have to fly in and drop stuff off every damn day."

Nick's parents didn't swear at all, so it shocked him to hear someone talk that way. His friend had several older brothers and sisters and all of his brothers were in the military. The older brother seemed like an adult to Nick, and not just an older brother.

"Those sorry fags flying them helos, they're like the damn taxi drivers of the whole war," the older brother said.

"Do they get shot down?" Nick asked.

"Hell, yeah," his brother said as he leaned toward Nick. "Then the gooks get a hold of them and put cigarettes out in their eyes."

Nick and his friend just stood there, letting that image wash over them. Then the brother started to laugh.

"You should see your damn faces!" he cackled.

"That ain't true?" Nick's friend asked.

"Hell, I don't know," the older brother said. He emptied the beer can and handed it to Nick's friend. "Everything over there is true at some point."

The older brother was only there for a day and then he was gone again and Nick's friend was alone except for his old, crabby mother.

The friend was always available to play, just like Nick, even though most of the other boys in the neighborhood had to go inside to eat or do homework.

Late in the evenings, the helicopters would drift away and it would be quiet. Nick and his friend would duck under the barbed wire and explore the field. None of the others boys would go out there for fear of getting in trouble.

On the other side of the huge field was another, much poorer, neighborhood. It was sometimes called "niggar town" by the older boys. Nick and his friend would kneel in the grass and watch the black children running along the edges of the field but they didn't get too close. They kept far enough away that they could get back to their side if they were being chased. The smell of burning tires would roll across the field in the winter and there was always the sound of barking dogs.

At his school, Nick kept away from the black kids as much as possible. They were on his bus, and they were always yelling and eating. Nick would sneak glances at them now and again. It was their hair that was so interesting. The black girls could style it differently from day to day so much so that Nick couldn't recognize them as the same person. The boys were sullen and mean, and they got in fights with each other often.

Nick had classes with them and they were often behind. Most of the work was copying down what the teachers would put on slides and project onto a screen. Nick could write fast so when he was done, he could turn his mind to something else while the other kids caught up.

For years, Nick had gone to school with a black boy that was quiet like him, and sad. His name was Michael. Michael was very quiet.

When he could, Nick sat next to Michael, and they would talk in low voices about things, and that is how Nick discovered that Michael loved comic books just as much as he did. Nick had lots of comic books and his dad would buy him a new one every time they went anywhere. Nick brought some to school to give to Michael and Michael was to bring some for Nick, but he never did.

Michael loved *Ritchie Rich*, the 'poor little rich boy' that was so nice to all his friends. Nick liked superhero comics like *The Justice League*, and he asked Michael if he had any new ones, but Michael did not. Michael lived with his grandmother and she didn't get many comics for him.

When they would talk in low tones, he would see Michael smile. On the bus, Michael did not smile and they never sat near each other. All of the kids on the bus, boys and girls, segregated themselves by skin color.

Nick kept his comic collection in good order and so he knew how many *Ritchie Rich* comics he had. There were a lot of them, more than he could carry to school. When he told Michael he wanted to give him more, but couldn't carry them all, Michael's eyes lit up.

Michael lived across the field where the helicopters came day after day, so they planned to meet on the field right after things grew quiet.

Nick was excited about giving so many comics to his friend. He found a plastic suitcase with a broken zipper in the garage and filled it with comics, mostly *Ritchie Rich* but also some *Archie*. He didn't care much for *Archie* anyway.

He zipped the suitcase shut, as much as the broken zipper would allow, and then he walked with it down the road towards the helicopter field. The suitcase was heavy with comics, but the field was only a few houses down.

When he reached the field, he could see a helicopter hovering in the distance. A few soldiers tumbled out on the ground, then after a moment, jumped up and rolled back inside the helicopter.

Finally, he saw, and then heard, the helicopter lifting off. He scanned the fence line on the other side of the field but didn't see Michael. He waited but still didn't see him. It was chilly and overcast and Nick hadn't put on a jacket, so he noticed for the first time that the wind was blowing and it was cold.

He sat down to wait and pulled out a comic. There was *Ritchie Rich* with his blond hair and little red bow tie. He was giving away a mansion to his girlfriend Gloria, and she was refusing to accept it.

He put that one away and pulled out another, and then another. When he looked up, he could see Michael at the fence line far away. Nick stood and waved his arms. Michael saw him and ducked under the barbed wire fence and started walking quickly his way.

Nick shoved the comics he was reading back into the suitcase and stepped under the barbed wire and then dragged the suitcase through and struggled to pick it up without dumping all the comics on the ground. It was harder this time since he was cold.

He could hear his feet crunching over the dead grass. He knew that when he got home, his shoelaces would be covered in tiny stickers that grew in the grasses of the field and would come off on his clothes and he'd jam them into his fingers when he undressed.

Michael started running as he came closer. A couple of times, Michael glanced furtively over his shoulder, back towards his neighborhood. He was out of breath when he reached Nick. Nick dropped the suitcase at Michael's feet.

"Wow," Michael said as he knelt down to look at the comics that had spilled out on the dead grass. A drop of sweat ran down his nose.

"It's mostly *Ritchie Rich*, and some *Archie*," Nick said proudly.

"OK, thanks," Michael said and wrapped his big, dark arms around the suitcase and stood. He turned and started to run back towards the fence line. Nick watched him until he reached the fence, stepped through the barbed wire with the suitcase hugged to his chest, and then disappeared into the woods.

Nick walked slowly back to the fence on his side. He was not in a hurry. It was nearly dark and getting colder, but he didn't have to go home and no one would come looking for him. It felt good to give something to someone, but he wished Michael had been a little more thankful.

That spring, Michael moved away from his grandmother's house and Nick didn't see him again. He had no other friends across the field on the other side where dogs bark continuously and the smell of burning tires filled the air.

The next time he saw Michael was when they were both in 9th grade and had started high school. Michael was a lot taller than Nick by then, and also many pounds heavier. He had a big afro and looked mean and walked the halls slowly with other black boys. When Nick passed him in the halls, Michael avoided eye contact, and they never spoke again.

PLAY MISTY

It was still dark when Dave arrived at Nick's house in the Gran Torino. Nick was waiting on the front porch with his trumpet case on his lap. He wasn't old enough to have a driver's license, and he was afraid of Dave's driving, but he had been to New Orleans before and nothing bad had happened. This time, he was going without his parents. He had less and less to say to his parents, anyway.

Nick liked Dave and liked that Dave was older, and could drive. Dave liked to get out and go places. Dave was tall and thin and goofy and usually in a good mood. He invited Nick to do things, and Nick always said yes.

Going to New Orleans had been Dave's idea, and he had put together the Dixieland combo they were taking. There would be two trumpet players, a trombone, and a tuba. Dave's idea was that they would play music on street corners and people would throw down money, and then they could eat and get drunk. As long as they were back for church the following morning, everything would be cool.

"My dad thinks I'm at your house," Dave said.

This alarmed Nick since he knew his parents would never lie to cover for anything.

"He won't call to check on you?" Nick asked.

"No," Dave said. "Plus, I don't think he knows your last name so he can't look up the number. He didn't ask about your house."

Nick thought about that for a moment. He never lied to his parents. They knew he was going to New Orleans but they didn't ask where he was staying or who he was going with or when he'd be back.

After a few minutes, Nick noticed that Dave was pulling into the parking lot of the K-mart.

"What are we doing here?" Nick asked, but before Dave could answer, Nick saw Misty getting out of her car.

"Bingo," Dave said under his breath. He turned to Nick and said, "She's going to ride up front, OK?"

Nick jumped over the front seat to the back. Misty opened the door and leaned over to kiss Dave. She was petite with long curly dark hair and watery blue eyes. Dave's attention was now focused entirely on Misty. Nick just looked out the window at the passing fields of dead grass that began to glow in the sunrise.

They passed the paper mill where Nick's dad worked and then drove into a neighborhood of trailers and shacks with asbestos shingles. Dave rolled down his window and the smell of smoke filled the car. It was cold and many homes had a fire going in their fireplace.

They stopped at a house and Dave honked the horn. Mark came through the screen door in an instant holding his trombone case and then he wedged into the back beside Nick. Misty smiled broadly at him. Mark wore black horn-rimmed glasses and was wearing a wool cap and he held his trombone case in his lap. Dave cracked a lot of jokes about Mark's blackness and Mark always laughed.

Dave talked to Mark but focused most of his attention on Misty. Nick didn't mind Misty being there, and watched her closely and wondered what she and Dave had done already. Mark made a lot of cracks about Misty and what Dave had done to her, and Dave made more cracks about Mark being black. They were having a good time.

They picked up the tuba player at a truck stop on I-10. His name was Dave as well, but everyone called him Potato Dave, so there was no confusion. He put the big tuba in the trunk of the Gran Torino.

Misty was the source of most of the attention for the rest of the drive to New Orleans. She sat sideways so she could talk to the boys in the back seat. Nick said very little. It started to get hot in the car so Dave rolled down his window and then Nick couldn't hear very much of what Misty was saying. After an hour, he fell asleep.

When the car slowed, he opened his eyes and saw they were in New Orleans. New Orleans was always the same. They parked on Esplanade and took their instruments out and warmed up their lips. It was a cold walk to Bourbon Street, and there weren't many people out. New Orleans didn't make much sense in the cold unless it was Mardi Gras. The entire suite of the senses, sight, sound, and smell, called out for a hot, buggy French Quarter.

Nick walked down the buckled sidewalks in silence. His hands were cold.

Finally, they stopped at Bourbon Street. Misty sat on the filthy broken sidewalk as Dave, Nick, Mark, and Potato Dave figured out where they wanted to stand. Dave was the leader, coming to New Orleans to play on street corners was his idea, and so he made the final decision. They stood in a line and after Dave counted off, they played "When the Saint Go Marching In" for the first time. Potato Dave fell behind, so Dave stopped them and they talked about tempo. Potato Dave said they were playing the song too fast, but Dave and Mark didn't think so.

Nick kept an eye on Misty. She caught him watching her and smiled. She had bright eyes and perfect teeth and he looked away quickly.

After they had played through "When the Saint Go Marching In" a few times, they tried out "Basin Street Blues" and then "Bill Bailey, Won't You Please Come Home." Dave played the melodies and Nick played the harmonies under him and the two trumpets blended nicely together. They had played these songs many times and knew them well. Mark played the trombone and he was easily the best musician of the bunch. Potato Dave fell into the rhythm and got louder and faster. When they moved to another spot and played "When the Saints Go Marching In" again, they fell into a groove, and the small crowd that gathered inspired them to play even more enthusiastically. Money was thrown down for them.

Dave counted the change in the trumpet case he had put out. There were five dollars and a bunch of dimes and pennies.

"We've only been here for about 15 minutes!" he said.

They packed up and moved down to Jackson Square and played "When the Saints Go Marching In" first, and then cycled through the whole set. They only knew six songs, so they would play them all and then take a break, allow those assembled to move on, and then play through them again for a new crowd.

In between sets, Dave would cross to Misty and kiss her. Nick observed as the kisses grew deeper and more intense as the sets passed by.

At sundown, they counted the money again and realized they had $85. It was enough to get something good to eat, so they went to Pat O'Brian's and ordered Po-boys for all. Dave ordered a 'Hurricane' and the bartender brought it to him. He gave most of it to Misty and she became quieter. After eating Po-boys, Mark wanted to get beignets, but Dave said he and Misty were going for a walk.

Nick loved New Orleans at night. He had been to New Orleans with his dad when he was a kid and his dad had kept him close, but Nick had seen the ladies who stood in the doorway of the strip clubs. They were called 'burlesques halls' then, or at least that's what his dad had called them. There was a topless woman on a swing that would swing out from the second floor of the club and then swing back inside. People would laugh and clap. As he and Mark and Potato Dave walked to Café Du Monde, he thought about how odd it was that his dad had brought him there when he was so young. Now he was there by himself, with no parents, and it was exciting.

They reached Café du Mont and it was not crowded. It was getting colder, and he didn't have a jacket, but the sweet little beignets and strong coffee warmed him. Mark and Potato Dave said that Dave was taking Misty to the car to have sex with her. Nick felt his stomach drop. He wondered what sex was like and if he would ever have sex with a girl like Misty. The road in his mind ended when thoughts of sex arrived. He just had no idea what it was like or what to imagine it was like or what to imagine it was like afterward.

They had plenty of money so they kept ordering more beignets and coffee. Potato Dave realized they had hot chocolate so they ordered some for all. The hot chocolate was sweet and delicious and Nick put his cold face right down next to the steam coming off the chocolate and breathed deep. He had never been so full or happy.

Misty and Dave found them an hour later. She was flushed and her neck and chest area were red. Dave was glassy-eyed and quiet but smiled even more than usual. Mark and Potato Dave giggled some and then ordered more beignets, coffee, and hot chocolate for Dave and Misty. Nick thought that Misty's face looked pale like she had seen a ghost.

They walked aimlessly around the French Quarter for a long time. After a while, there weren't many people on Bourbon Street, and everyone who was still out was drunk and yelling or staggering or just sitting down. The police were out and several were on horseback. Dave got more 'Hurricanes' and gave them to Mark and Potato Dave. A man staggered by and called Mark a 'stinking niggar.' Mark laughed but Dave pushed the man and a fight almost happened. Misty and Mark told Dave to let it go, the guy was a drunk as well as an asshole, and they were having fun.

After a long while, Misty looked tired. When Dave, Mark, and Potato Dave left to get one more 'Hurricane,' Nick sat on the curb next to her and she lay her head on his shoulder. He quietly breathed deep and could smell her. She smelled like flowers and sweat. His mind scrambled, trying to think of something to say.

"Are you OK?" he asked.

"I'm fine," she said without opening her eyes. "But you're so sweet to ask."

The guys came back a few minutes later and announced they were out of money.

On the way home, everyone except Dave slept. Misty laid her head down in Dave's lap and Mark let his head fall back and his mouth dropped open. Potato Dave curled up and didn't make a sound. Dave rolled his window down and told Nick he needed the cold to keep him awake. They had about three hours to get home before he had to go to church.

Nick slept a little, but he would wake and breathe deep, trying to retrieve the smell he had smelled when they first got in the car. It was earthy and tangy and smelled of a woman, but not in a way he knew. No one said anything, but he knew it was something to do with Dave and Misty. It went away quickly and didn't return.

Nick didn't see Dave much after that except at band practice. They would talk while the band director was yelling at the wind players and the flag girls. When breaks came, Dave would cross to Misty and they would mesh fingers and kiss. She was always with him on breaks and she left with him in his car after practice so Nick got a ride home with another friend, one he didn't like as much.

OVER THE EDGE

Thirty months of high school was plenty. Later, Nick wouldn't remember if he had talked to his parents or not about leaving high school. Surely he did; they must have signed something but he couldn't remember.

On the day he went to the testing center to test out of high school, he had driven himself. He drove himself everywhere from the day he had a license. He drove himself to get his teeth pulled. He drove himself to the emergency room. The driver's license had ended his relationship with his parents.

Nick assembled with the others in a large room and sat down. Moments later, Suzanne sat down in the seat in front of him and turned around.

He was happy to see someone he knew. And, he was happy it was her. Twenty-four months earlier, she had been a flat-chested freshman and he was shy and awkward, but they had become friends. In class, she sat behind him so he would turn around at his desk to talk to her, and she smiled. Now, she was sitting in front of him, and she was about to step over the threshold at the same time he was. They were leaving high school behind. They were ending their public education process early to show that they had had quite enough. She told him she wanted to work more and didn't have many friends in school anyway. He said he was bored and ready to start college.

They listened to the instructions, everyone was given a number two pencil, and then the tests were passed out. Whatever they were doing, it was starting now.

A week later, he found out he had passed. A high school diploma was mailed to his house. The next day he went around to his teachers and triumphantly asked for their signature that released him from class. He was only 16 and barely a junior, but he was out of high school.

A few weeks later, he broke up with his high school girlfriend. She had been his first kiss, his first relationship, and his first fumbling sexual encounters without actual sex. The relationship ended with her running into her house in tears. Lacking that reinforcing bond of seeing each other every day in school, they were done.

That cleared the way for the call to Suzanne. She answered on the second ring and accepted his invitation to meet for pizza.

Suzanne was from a poor family. Her dad had been killed in Vietnam and her mother lived in a tiny home on a dirt road. Her brothers were often in trouble, and her mother was overwhelmed. And so, like Nick, Suzanne was on her own at a young age. She worked at McDonald's to pay for her car.

They meet at a pizza parlor a few nights later and talked and talked.

Suzanne had a friend whose parents were never home. Suzanne and Denise met in Kindergarten. Denise's dad was in the Navy and had 19 spent most of his adult life at sea. Nick never met her friend's dad and met her mom only once as she headed out to her job at a liquor store.

Most of the time, Nick and Suzanne met at Denise's house to watch TV, but even Denise wasn't there. Denise spent most of her time with her boyfriend, so Nick and Suzanne were alone most of the time.

Alone in that home, a place where neither was in the daylight, they marched onward physically. He touched her breasts, first over her shirt, and then under her shirt but over her bra, then under her bra. She marched forward on his body as well, grabbing his cock first over his pants, then down his pants, and finally, with his pants open.

When summer came, Nick developed a routine of college classes in the morning, the gym after lunch, and then the beach in the late afternoon, and then he'd meet Suzanne at Denise's house. The other students in his classes were all much older, so he made no friends there. The guys at the gym were older as well. He went to the beach alone and lay in the sun alone. He thought a lot about getting back to Denise's house where he would meet Suzanne.

They moved to other places in the house. They went to the hall bathroom where she put his cock in her mouth. She took some time to get used to it, and he had to quietly say "No teeth," a couple of times.

They moved to Denise's room where they would push the piles of laundry off the bed to lay down. There, they would use their hands on each other and then lay entwined. The day of complete sex, after so many years of thinking about it, so many years of looking at girls and wondering what they were like, what they were all about, wondering what it was like to possess one, was at hand.

But while his body was in motion, his mind was stepping on the brake, and as the moment was getting closer, his mind was pressing the brake harder. He wanted to move forward, and he didn't.

His parents were religious and he had attended church until his mother had freaked out and rejected the Baptists. His father went along with whatever his mother wanted. They stopped going to church, but Nick accepted the Bible as doctrine anyway. He had nothing else. The warnings about sex were evident enough throughout the Bible.

There was also a drumbeat of messages about "teen pregnancy" and "unwanted pregnancy." At his high school, flyers hung on every wall about the dangers of sex. Teachers would speak about teenagers and sex as if it was a horrible sort of Russian roulette of peril with pregnancy as the bullet to the head of "your future." Based on what he had heard, an abortion clinic was the only alternative, but it was a stigma that lasted a lifetime as well.

He was fearful. He told Suzanne that he didn't want to be "out of control."

One evening, they had both lay in Denise's bed, she was completely nude and so was he, but he didn't have sex with her. She used her hand, and he came and got dressed.

After a time, they broke up. There was no precipitating factor; just a short fight and a breakup and no more returned calls.

It took a few days, but eventually, a pain came over him that he had never known and didn't know was possible. He longed for her. He thought of her constantly. Brief phone conversations that seemed normal would soothe him, but then, the pain would return. He ached from the moment he woke up until he went to bed and he would put off trying to call her until he had told himself it was OK, but more often than not, she didn't answer.

Nick put in a lot more time at the gym. The older men in the gym were funny. They swapped diet tips and training tips and lay in the sun behind the building to develop their tans. The guys trained hard and the bigger ones would enter bodybuilding contests and bring back trophies.

Nick liked the guys at the gym and wanted to be like them. They seemed so relaxed and easy. But, they were older and had lives of their own and he knew he couldn't be friends with them. None would be mentors to him or "take him under their wing" like in the movies. He was on his own.

His appearance continued to change. He measured his muscles regularly and the difference between his chest and his waist was growing. The sense of being in control of his body made him lightheaded with joy. He decided that if he could control this part of his life, he could control all of it.

He drifted back to Suzanne eventually, but she was different. She had different clothes, wore her hair differently, and she moved into an apartment of her own. She no longer worked fast food and was a real waitress at a nice restaurant. In her apartment, they drifted quickly back into the same physical pattern. He was there during the day hours, so he could see her body clearly. The march toward sex was back on.

In her bedroom, as she masturbated him, he pushed her backward, she lay down, and he slipped into her. He entered with no resistance. He moved it back and forth twice and then pulled backward and spewed on her pelvis. Afterward, she got up and went to the bathroom and he got dressed.

"I think we're still virgins, right?" he asked, but she didn't answer.

After that, the phone went unanswered. He would meet her, but she didn't invite him back to her apartment.

And then he found out that she was dating a much older guy. Johnny was older and worked for a liquor distributor. Nick knew Johnny through his sister. Johnny was in his twenties and Nick could do the math on what was happening.

He could not avoid concluding what the facts dictated which was that Suzanne had moved on and was having sex with other guys. He knew it, he knew it in his heart, and it sickened him. The thought of it made a physical sensation in his stomach so clearly that he could point to the spot where it was happening.

He went back to thinking of her without ceasing. He drove past her apartment and looked up at the bedroom window. It was dark most of the time.

After a few days, he couldn't stand it anymore. He knocked on her door. The sun was low, and the hallway outside of her apartment was lit with a yellow bulb that had no cover. After a long time, and a few knocks, she answered the door. Her hair was messy and she was wearing shorts and a low-cut top. He entered quickly and saw a man sitting on the couch. It was Johnny.

Time stopped. He could see it on her and smell it in the air. He had interrupted something. It was something he knew. Johnny was going to bed with her soon.

After some quiet words and glances at the floor, he left. He felt as if he had been kicked in the stomach. Had he been closer with the funny guys at the gym, he would have gone to them and laughed, but he wasn't. There was no one. He couldn't go to his parents.

He drove around for a while. Then he had to pull over because he couldn't see. His eyes filled with tears so thick that it was like he was underwater. On the side of the road, he wept deeply for a while. He rested his head on the steering wheel and cried.

After some time, he stopped. The crying had made his stomach feel better. Now there was just the cold realization of what had happened, and his need to adjust to it. So, in his mind, he decided. After thinking on it further, he decided even harder. Then he decided so hard he said it out loud.

"I tried to be good, and look what I got," he said. He thought more. "God, you screwed me!" he said aloud as he drove. No tears now; only clenched teeth. "This is bullshit!" he said out loud.

The final part was settled in his mind and he didn't say it out loud. From this day forward, he knew, any opportunities with a woman would be taken. He would not say no again, not ever.

SHIT BUCKET

"**H**ey, man, do you have a bucket I can use?"

The dude in front of me had long, curly blond hair and was rail-thin with hairy arms, but he was one of the friendly ones. I had seen him before, and he was usually smiling. Smiling sort of made him stand out from the rest of the men on the rig. I'd see them all, standing at the railing outside the dorm, smoking and tossing the butts down to the oily water below. The water around the rig had a light sheen of oil on it and reflected a rainbow of colors. Most of the men never smiled, talked very little, and would space themselves out along the rail so they could be alone.

But, not this guy. He was friendly, and he talked, so I wanted to help him. I was standing in the galley kitchen and, upon his request, started looking around for a bucket.

I didn't need a job that bad, but I took this one so I could get away from my parent's house. It was boring there, and the guys in my neighborhood were assholes. I needed a break from all of them. Plus, I like the water. Starring at the horizon takes the edge off that great sea sickness called life, so the idea of being able to see the water no matter which way I turned my head was appealing.

Also, I knew guys who had been out on the rigs and they were who I wanted to be. I thought working on the rigs would sound impressive to girls and I'd be able to say things like "Hey, did you put gas in your car today? Someone had to go out and get the oil that made the gas, and that's what I do." It would sound cool and it would be cool. I would have graduated. I'd be a full-grown man.

I got an application from a buddy and I filled it out and he took it back with him to the rig office. The next time he came home, he told me I was hired, and all I had to do was go back with him to Belle Chase and sign up. They'd send me out the same day.

The night before we left, we shot some pool with the girls, and then I went back to my girl's house and we took a shower together. Afterward, we moved to the bed but she was cold so we couldn't leave the covers off the way I liked. We had sex and the space under the covers filled with the smell of her sex. I liked that smell. Later, when she was gone, it was her scent I missed most. Where I was going was filled with smells I'd miss as well once they were gone, but I didn't know that yet.

On the way to Belle Chase, my friend talked constantly about football, and then girls, and then his dad, and then some other stuff. I thought about my girlfriend a lot and some of the lies I had told her. God, what a jackass I could be, I thought.

But now, I was going to work out on the rigs with the real men. Talk time was over. I was a little afraid, but my friend had been there, and if he could hack it, I knew I could, too. There was just no point in being scared of anything anymore.

When we got to Belle Chase, I saw the boat that would take us out to the rigs. It wasn't nearly as big as I thought it would be. I had water skied behind boats that size. Maybe the rigs weren't that far out, I thought, but I was wrong. Inside the office, there was a map that showed where every rig was located and my friend pointed to the one where we were going. It was a long way to the mouth of the Mississippi River and then another 45 miles straight out. We were taking that little boat way out into the Gulf of Mexico.

As I filled out the paperwork, I thought about Mark Twain. No one I knew read very much, so there wasn't anyone to talk to about such things. I read *Tom Sawyer*, and now I was going to get a little time on the Mississippi River, just like Tom. That excited me, and I wanted to say something to someone, but looking around the room, and seeing the faces, I knew that it would be a bad idea to talk about books. So, I kept my mouth shut.

I turned my paperwork in and was given a plastic ID badge. "Don't lose that damn badge," the guy behind the counter told me. "You got to turn it in when you get back to get your damn paycheck, so don't lose it." I stuck the badge in my duffel bag like my friend did and he told me no one would ever ask for it and he was right. No one ever did.

We got on the boat and moved up to the front and then sat down on our duffel bags with our backs to the bow. The boat had no seats and no bimini top over the steering wheel. It was powered by two outboard motors and the crosshatch of the fiberglass hull was visible through the worn paint on the deck. My friend grew quiet as the other men started to board.

I began to get a good look at the guys we'd be working with. They were all big, with thick waists and wrinkled, tanned skin. Nearly all of them lit a cigarette after they dropped their bags on the deck. A couple of them greeted each other with some Creole slang that I didn't understand. None were black, but one was Mexican, and he didn't speak to anyone. Having no black men was unusual for a laboring job out of Louisiana. I started to ask my friend about this but decided not to.

Once the big engines started, my friend could talk to me without anyone hearing him. He leaned in and yelled into my ear.

"Take a look around at their hands and count how many fingers are missing," he said.

I looked around and counted six missing fingers. There were 8 guys, so out of 80 fingers, 6 were missing.

"I count six," I said.

"I count 13," he said. "You got to look close. Some just lost the tip. Those are all roughnecks. They're mostly cool and they do the important stuff. The rest are roustabouts, and most of them are cool, but some are crazy and they play jokes on everyone. If they're missing a finger, they're a roughneck."

"We're the only galley hands?" I asked.

"Yeah, the two that are out there will take the boat back, and we'll take their place," he said.

I stood up to get a good look at the Mississippi River. It was as I had always imagined it; broad and muddy and magnificent. Had there been someone to talk to, I would have had a lot to say. But my friend had crossed his arms and closed his eyes. I saw egrets and cranes on the shore, and then seagulls. The salty smell of the Gulf of Mexico was in my nose.

After a while, the water started to get rough, and up ahead, I could see the river widening and split off into multiple paths. It wasn't clear which one was the main current of the river but then I noted the markers and, as we steered to the right, I saw a huge oceangoing freighter up ahead. It was massive, with four cranes on the deck. I kicked my friend and he looked over the side at the approaching ship but then crossed his arms again and closed his eyes.

When we passed the big ship, the men on our boat yelled a few things at the men who were smoking along the railing of the freighter and there was lots of laughter. One of the men on the big boat dropped his pants and mooned us. Another man started to spank the man who was mooning us.

After that, I had to sit down since the water was getting choppy and spray was coming over the bow. The pilot didn't slow down at all. The rest of the men shifted position and tried to get as close to the bow as possible so the spray would go over them and land on the men who sat at the stern.

In another hour, the pilot slowed and I looked up to see the brown river water giving way to the deep blue of the open ocean. There were still narrow spits of land visible behind us but we were coming into the Gulf of Mexico. Rolling swells were visible on the horizon.

"How much further from here?" I asked my friend.

"A while," he said. "Try to sleep because we're going to have to go to work for 16 hours as soon as we get there."

I pulled my shirt up over my chin and felt my hot breath on my face. That always comforted me. None of the other men did much except cross their arms, but I didn't care. The thought of 16 straight hours of work was sobering. After a while, I did fall asleep and I woke only a few times when we'd hit a big swell or I heard someone yelling over the throb of the engines.

When the engines slowed way down, I knew we were there. I looked over the bow railing and there it was. Everything looked just like the pictures my friend had shown me.

The rig was high off the water. From the water to the top of the crane was 120 feet but the main deck was 60 feet off the surface and supported by three towers. The platform formed a sort of star suspended between three steel columns that had a high deck and a crane perched in the middle. It was a fantastic sight and I will never forget the first time I saw it.

We came closer and I saw a mesh platform below the main rig housing on the nearest column. There were men on it and they had duffel bags on their shoulders, so I figured they were going home. This platform was 20 feet off the water and as we came closer still, one of the guys on the platform climbed down a metal ladder built into one of the huge pilings.

I could see what a trick this was going to be. The swells were rolling past and rising up the huge rusty steel columns a solid five feet up and down so even if the platform had been lower, we wouldn't be able to step off on it. The only way off the boat and to the rig was to grab the rungs of the ladder and climb up to the platform.

No one said anything as the men stood and hefted their duffels onto their shoulders. Everyone on the boat was wet and quiet. The boat pilot came forward and pulled a rope out from a hatch in the deck and laid it out neatly then went back to the wheel. No one moved to help him.

We came under the platform. The men above were smoking, of course, and they flicked their butts into the water around us which I could see had a thin sheen of oil that reflected a rainbow of light. No one seemed concerned that it might catch on fire.

Everything moved very fast then. The pilot slowed the boat just as we reached the massive piling, then he came forward and threw the line to the guy who had climbed down, and that guy tied us off with the bowline. The pilot cut the big motors and it was very quiet except for the lapping sounds of water.

After a moment, the current pointed us downwind. The pilot came forward and grabbed the bowline and pulled us in so we were just a few feet from the ladder rungs. We all formed a line behind the first man who lined up beside the pilot.

The pilot pulled the boat towards the piling until the bow touched and then the first man off the boat made the short leap to the ladder. He did it smoothly and then was up the ladder in an instant. The next man did it the same way. A swell came past and the boat was pushed away from the piling, so the guy who followed waited until the pilot had pulled the boat close again, then he made the step.

I was nervous about that big step and didn't want to fall into the water. My friend went first, and I went right after him. I should have waited until he was higher up the ladder because a big swell came through but I could move up, and so the water rose to my knees. Still, I didn't fall and no one said anything.

We climbed up to the platform, walked across a metal bridge to another piling, and then climbed another metal ladder and went through a door that housed a set of metal stairs.

The next hour was a swirl of faces and hallways and a few minutes in a large dorm filled with bunk beds. I stood my duffel in a locker and followed my friend to the kitchen where a big black man named Cue Ball clamped my friend in a bear hug. He shook my hand soul style and made some comments I didn't understand but he was smiling and I liked that. I wanted this man to approve of me and so I acted eager to get to work.

The next several hours were spent in the same space at the back of the kitchen prepping food for Cue Ball and doing dishes that my friend handed back to me. Recipes were posted on the walls and I had to read them, go to pantry racks along the side wall or into the huge walk-in cooler and bring out the ingredients. I would assemble them and do whatever my friend told me I had to do.

"Open all the yams and put them in that big mixing bowl and add in the brown sugar. Don't put in too much; just follow the directions," he said.

He told me all the recipes were ones that Cue Ball knew well and so if anything was off, he'd know, and he'd get pissed and throw things.

Men came and went from the small dining hall just beyond Cue Ball's serving window. We put the pot roast, turkey, sweet potatoes, green beans, and pudding out in metal bins, and then I brought back piles of dirty dishes and ran them through the dishwasher. There were no windows in the kitchen or the dining hall so I hadn't seen the water for hours. It was easy to forget that you were way out in the Gulf of Mexico and not in a cafeteria kitchen in Nebraska.

After cooking, cleaning, and serving food for several hours, my friend showed me the laundry area. It was down a hall behind the big walk-in cooler. There were eight industrial washing machines and eight dryers lined up in a row in a room with a low ceiling.

The laundry method was simple; if a man wanted something washed, he'd put it in a mesh bag and hang the bag on a hook by his bed. Every bag had a cloth tag with a number written on it. Every four hours, we'd pass through the dorm and collect the bags. We threw the bags in the washer, then put them through the dryer, and then back on the hook. Everything was washed in hot water so we never touched the settings on the washer or dryer. Nothing was folded. We just collected bags, washed and dried what was in them, and took them back. If a man didn't want his clothes or his sheets washed, that was his business.

We worked through the night prepping food and passing in and out of the dorm with mesh bags of laundry. At midnight, Cue Ball told us to go to bed. We went out on the deck outside the dorm and looked up at the stars. The sky was alive with points of light. The air was thick with the smell of salt and the black water below was sloshing past the pilings of the platform and it made a comforting rumble. I was tired but had never felt so good.

I had been out for five days when the skinny guy asked me for the bucket. He was looking around the kitchen area, and seemed a little jittery. Something on his body was always moving. He swiveled his head around, waved his arms side to side, and shifted his weight back and forth. I had emptied a bucket of pickles earlier in the day so I went back to the cooler and found the bucket. When I held it up so he could see it, he said "Perfect!"

"I'll find the lid for it," I said, and started to look around.

"No, man, I don't need a lid," he said. "See, what we're going to do is we're going to shit in this bucket, and then we're going to slide it up under Mike D's bed. When he lays down, he'll go fucking crazy trying to figure out where the shit smell is coming from."

"More than one of you is going to shit in the same bucket?" I said.

'Yeah, man. We all shit in the same toilets; they're just big buckets," he said. I had never thought about it that way.

"Thanks, man," he said and left the kitchen.

"Get the fuck out of my kitchen," I heard Cue Ball say as the skinny guy passed.

An hour later, I headed for the dorm to round up mesh bags, and I saw the skinny guy and two other guys, both roustabouts, peaking into the dorm. They were holding back laughs and the skinny guy had to cover his mouth with his stained hand to keep from making noise. When he saw me, he motioned for me to be quiet and come over.

"He's in his bed and he's tossing and turning around. Funny as shit!" he whispered to me.

I looked in and saw Mike D in his bed. Mike D was short, bald, and thick. He was on his back and while his eyes were closed, he was making a face. He was awake and he smelled shit.

"Go in and get his laundry bag! Tell us if you smell it," the skinny guy said to me.

I entered the room and started to collect bags. The whole room was shitted up. Suddenly, a man in one of the top bunks sat up.

"Fucking Mike D, did you shit yourself? Jesus Christ!" he said. It was hard not to laugh because I could hear the guys in the hall laughing. If I started laughing, they'd blame me for ruining their joke, so I kept a straight face.

Suddenly, Mike D jumped up and I had no trouble not laughing because he was pissed.

"What the fuck!" he yelled. "Someone has smeared shit on something or they shit in their bed or something."

He looked at me.

"Do any of those bags smell like shit?" he asked.

I lifted the bags and sniffed them. I heard the skinny guy stifle a squeal but Mike D didn't notice. The bags smelled like stale sweat and grease and cigarette smoke.

"No, sir," I said and continued on.

I collected Mike D's bag and got a solid whiff of what he smelled and it was truly foul. I held my breath and headed for the door.

In the hallway, the skinny guy and the other two were red-faced and covering their mouths, and doubled over. The skinny guy patted me on the back. I went on to the laundry room.

A few minutes later, I saw all the men on the balcony. Mike D had found the bucket. All of them were laughing, even Mike D. They all looked in the bucket and laughed some more. Mike D heaved the shit-filled bucket out to sea.

I worked a total of four shifts that summer; two weeks on, and then two weeks off. My friend stopped getting along with Cue Ball, and so Cue Ball made me his favorite. He moved me forward and my friend back to the prep station so he had to wash dishes. That pissed my friend off so we saw each other less when we were onshore. On the last shift I worked that summer, I had to drive myself to Belle Chase.

The skinny guy was back for a while, but I found out he was picked up in New Orleans for a parole violation and had to go back to jail. I made friends with most of the guys who were regulars. They were easy to talk to and simple in what they wanted. I did my job steadily and never complained and that was what they respected. Nothing any of us did was that hard.

I got used to the routine and so the job was very easy and I always enjoyed the nights on the rig, even when my friend wouldn't go out on the rails with me anymore. The sky was always thick with stars unless it was raining. I could see the long arc of the Milky Way rise from the dark waters. When the moon was full, it was so bright you could read by the light.

The guys played more jokes on each other until Cue Ball mounted a TV on the wall in the dining hall. It came with a tape deck and so they played a lot of movies on it. For some reason, that cut down on the pranks. Guys would sit in the dining hall and watch movies when they weren't working.

I saw hundreds of shooting stars when I was out leaning on the rails. The guys were always out there smoking and looking down at the dark waters. It was like being alone even though 30 men were living in a metal box together. They didn't speak much to each other, much less a galley hand like me.

But what I wanted, to be graduated to full-grown manhood, was done. I never used my snappy lines on any girls, because now I didn't have to. I talked a lot less overall and I stopped lying so much.

After our last shift, I said goodbye to my friend in the parking lot in Belle Chase. He was still pissed at me but I didn't make an issue of it. It turned out to be the last time I saw him. That Christmas, he got drunk and ran his car off the road and hit a tree. He lived for a few days but died just past the New Year. When summer came, I couldn't bear to go back out there without him even though he had been an asshole to me at the end of his life. It was sad that my full-grown manhood was going to last a lot longer than his. I certainly didn't deserve it.

LEAVING IT ALL BEHIND

African music is all drumming and singing, with little harmony. The dancing is done from the hips. It is a blunt art form and, by design, takes up a lot of time. Nick thought it was genius that the drumming had very easy parts that anyone could do, and then a drummer could be apprenticed up to the lead drummer who banged out a complex series of patterns that were just cool as hell.

Nick knew he could dance. Some people could, some people could not, and Nick could. He could make his torso pop and he could move his feet. Not as well as the girls, but he could do it.

A long, multi-hour class in African music and dance was the perfect way to end a day at art school. Nick had not yet figured out how precious his time really was. The African teachers were deep blue black with thick accents and the students were mostly upper class white kids, all young and eager to learn, and a few black kids looking to find roots they never had. The male students were mostly drummers, except for Nick. The girls were a mixed bag of dancers and female musicians attracted to the dance because it was easy and sexual and they liked dancing in front of the line of guys.

Celia was the best of them all, and the other dancers deferred to her. She was small, bony, and delicate, and unlike the other dancers, she wore fashionable clothes with no rips. She moved and acted like a real dancer, and whatever dance move she was shown, she did it perfectly with no further practice or instruction.

Celia had brown skin that shown like a sandy wood rubbed for hours with olive oil. Her thick hair was pulled back tight which exposed her high forehead and tiny features. She was the shortest of the female dancers but she captured everyone's attention. In a room full of good-looking art school hippy chicks, she stood out as well-dressed and professional.

By the third class, they began to acknowledge each other and the flirting began. Nick still had a cold feeling deep in his heart, a feeling that he was alone and far outside his element, but flirting with a girl was natural, and he excelled at it. He had only been in California a few months and the dislocation was still acute. Lining up new dates made things seem more normal.

He thought she was wealthy, and he was right. After a few short conversations, he found out she was a native Angeleno, and close to graduation. She took the African music classes because she liked them, and it was relaxing relative to her ballet classes. She wasn't even there for credit and the teachers didn't care.

He could not ask Celia on a date since he had basically nothing. He didn't have money, he didn't have a car, and even if he did, he wouldn't know where he was going. He had arrived at the airport, taken a bus north, and after a time where the city faded away, arrived at the college. He was barely aware of where he was. It had been months, and he had spent a lot of time alone. It had been an interesting time, and he had met some cool people, but the core loneliness persisted.

He had knocked off a couple of girls already. One had been a voice student from San Francisco. They had gone into a class room during a party and had sex on a desk.

The other had been a dancer with odd hair who had moved down from Vancouver. They had sex in the dorms on her single bed with the light on. Afterwards, he rolled off her and reached up the turn the light off.

"I'm going to have to ask you to leave," she said. His arm froze in mid-air.

"Me?" he said, looking over his shoulder at her.

She said she had to get up early the next morning and was ready for bed so he needed to leave. He went back to his room and noted that he still had sweat on himself from their encounter. When he told one of his new friends what had happened, the guy laughed.

"Yeah, California girls aren't like what you're used to," he said.

"Normally, if you make it back to her place, sex includes breakfast," he said incredulously. "I think I've been fucked!"

That had been a weeks ago. He had settled his eye on a few new fillies to carve away from the herd but there were so many to choose from. Art school was easy hunting for Nick.

Finally, when there was no one else close, Celia asked him a question.

"So, how do you like it in LA?" she said. Her tone suggested that he would say something negative about the city. The natives loved to complain about Los Angeles.

"What I saw coming from the airport looked OK," he said. "That's all I was able to see."

"You haven't been down to the city yet?" she asked.

"I haven't been off the campus except to the deli down the hill," he said. He hoped this conversation was going to go where he wanted it to.

"That is just not right," she said.

Bingo.

She said she would pick him up that Friday and she would show him Los Angeles. For the rest of the week, he thought about Friday, and what would happen. Since the heart break period of his teen years, he had learned to read women well, and he knew this was a date, not just a sightseeing tour. And, if it was a date, he would be on point. He would know how to act, he would be at his most attuned, and he would mold his conversation exactly to hers, responding to each thing she said with attention and seriousness. It would go well.

The rest of the week dragged past with Friday at the end of time. He said nothing about the date to anyone.

She arrived at the dorm in a black Mercedes. The Mercedes emblem on the hood was one of the most recognized brands in the world and universally associated with wealth and glamour, and she drove it smoothly and comfortably. Several people in the lobby watched as he went out and climbed into the Mercedes. There would be questions when he returned.

She was dressed in white linen which made her mahogany skin stand out even more. She was lightly perfumed and wore a tiny gold chain around her neck. After he got in the big Mercedes, she kissed his cheek and they left campus.

"So this is the 405 and we're going through the famous Valley, which you've probably heard of," she said. Celia had a lilting singsong vocal manner that was unique.

"Where do you live?" he asked.

"In the Valley, in Encino" she said, laughing. "I'm a Val, born and raised."

Nick fished through the cassette tapes she had in a case until he found a classical jazz selection. They listened as they drove through the Sepulveda pass towards the beach.

First, she took him to Venice Beach, where he saw with his own eyes, the places he had been seeing in photos since he was a pre-teen. Nick had been lifting weights since he was a freshman in high school and he had pictures of Arnold Schwarzenegger on his bedroom walls. And now, he was looking at Gold's Gym.

Next, they went to Santa Monica and she parked so they could look at the ocean and walk out on the Santa Monica Pier. The sky was starting to run through an array of oranges and reds and then deep blues. As they crossed through Palisades Park, he saw men in suits lying down at the base of huge palm trees.

"Only in LA would business people take a nap in a park," he said.

She looked away from the ocean to what he was seeing.

"Those aren't business people. Those are homeless people. They live here," she chuckled.

"Look; they have suits. That one has a brief case," he said.

"That was for the Olympics. They didn't want the homeless looking so scary so they gave them new clothes," she said. "Wait a few more weeks and they'll be back to normal.

When the sun hit the water, they headed to Hollywood. They drove down Hollywood Boulevard, and passed landmarks which she pointed out to him. There was the Chinese Theater, the Columbia Records building, the Crossroads of the World, The Whiskey a Go-Go, and the Roxy. Some of the things she pointed out as landmarks he didn't know about. He knew he wanted to go to them, and he wanted her to take him.

She decided that he would have Thai food for the first time. When they reached Chan Dara, she couldn't find a parking place. Finally, something he could do.

"You go on in and I'll find a place to park," he said authoritatively.

They switched seats, and he dropped her off in front of the restaurant, and drove the huge Mercedes around the block. It felt fantastic. He found a spot a few blocks away. He was careful to head back on foot the way he came and not get lost.

When he reached the restaurant, he could see her inside sitting by herself. It was early, and there were still many empty tables. She was a vision of beauty and exotic California sophistication. She was looking down, reading the menu, and he stared for a moment at her hair, neck, and hands.

He watched her, and then looked down the broad boulevard to the stop lights and the hills beyond. Traffic throbbed past in a whirl, and he could smell the fumes from the cars idling at the stop light at the end of the block. Everything was a sea of tail lights, neon, and soothing urban background noise. He could hear the radio from the passing cars. Chatter came from a million directions.

He knew this night would end well. It might even include breakfast. Finally, he knew how this game was played. He had mastered something.

But right now, this was the signal, the sign, the omen that he had left some things behind. He was far away from home, from his Mother, from his dad, from the smallness and insignificance of life away from what he had seen on TV. Everything he had ever seen in the movies or read about in a magazine was right there in front of him.

He took a final breath. He was high as a kite. Nick knew he would never die.

THE HOTTEST SUMMER EVER

The plan was to travel at night because Laura's legs would swell in the heat, and while Nick knew she wasn't fully aware of just how far they were about to drive, he knew. I-10 stretched out across the country in a long, flat line that passed through the hottest places in the whole country, and Nick had experienced the route several times already. He knew, and she did not, that they were driving into a furnace.

She was not sturdy, stoic, or even very nice, but she was funny. He wanted her to come with him, he wanted to share what he knew, but he also knew that she would complain along the way, and traveling by day in his truck, which was black and had no air conditioner, was just a bad idea. He wasn't keen on a day trip through Texas either, so he announced that they would leave late in the afternoon and travel mostly by night. She didn't care since she planned on reading or sleeping most of the way.

A week before they were to leave, he started packing up boxes of things he wanted to store at his parent's home back in Florida. There were heavy boxes of record albums that were beloved, as well as some clothes and blankets that he had slowly brought to California over the years and planned to return to his mother. Laura made no prep plans and added her clothes to his suitcase at the last minute.

He stopped by the library to return some books and saw Gary reading the newspaper. Gary had to move as well since the summer was coming to an end.

"Remember that big board you used up in Ventura?" he asked. "You can have it since I don't have any more room."

Nick brought Gary's big surfboard back to his dorm room. Laura was sitting on the sofa in her bra and eating a cheese sandwich as he walked in with the board.

"Gary pawned that old thing off on you, I see," she said. "I knew he would." She worked in the library and had slept with Gary a long time ago.

"I used this board before. This is called a log," he said defensively.

"I know what a log is," she said. "I'm from Venice Beach. That's a cheap board."

He looked closer at the board; it was cheap. She was right and he shouldn't have taken it. But, he did, and he wasn't going to reverse the decision.

Days passed with little to do. In the evenings, before it got dark, they went to empty dorm rooms and had sex on the floor, or sometimes on the mattresses that had no sheets. During the day, they went to the movie theater where there was air conditioning and saw two movies, and ate popcorn in the lobby. She was always funny. Her humor was based on sarcasm and mocking imitations of other people, often of him, but she did it well.

As summer was nearing the end, the heat intensified. It was time to make the drive, so he quit his bartending job and she finished her job at the library, and they finished packing.

The morning they were to leave, he drove his truck to the loading dock at the dorm and started loading boxes in the bed of his truck. His old roommate arrived in his girlfriend's car and watched for a while. Gary came by, and a couple of Laura's friends. No one offered to help, and they asked no questions. Most conversations revolved around how Laura would take to the road and ended with "Well, good luck!" She was a known quantity.

While no one asked about what would happen on the long drive if it rained, Nick had thought about it a lot. He had a nylon tarp which he planned to wrap around everything once it was all packed. He had ropes and would tie everything down after the tarp was laid over things and then top the whole thing off with the surfboard. That was the plan.

Laura slept most of the morning and then made breakfast and smoked a few cigarettes. Her clothes were packed, and they had taken the rest of her things back to her parents' house the previous weekend.

The day with her parents in Venice Beach was uncomfortable. Nick didn't understand the issue between her and her dad. When they were driving away, her dad was knocking on the passenger side window to say goodbye, but she looked away and wouldn't roll the window down. Nick didn't know if he should pull away or not. After a few uncertain seconds, her dad gave up and Nick drove away.

After loading all of the boxes, Nick took the surfboard to the truck. Laura gathered up what little she was taking. It was time to go.

Tying the surfboard to the truck was more difficult than he had anticipated. It had no hooks or obvious places to tie off to and wrapping it several times with rope was the best he could do. The tip of the board extended over the cab of the truck.

No one was there when they left. The dorm cast a long afternoon shadow over the truck as they pulled away.

Even though he had filled up the gas tank on the truck, he had to stop so she could get a drink and another pack of cigarettes.

"So, you know I'm going to have to pee like, every stop, so don't be like my dad when I do," she said as she climbed back in.

"So, you know we're driving to Florida, and it takes a long time, right?" he asked.

She smiled. Her smile was the one thing he really, truly liked about her that was unequivocal. On many days, she smiled and genuinely seemed happy. She had many other phases and was a bundle of things he would come to know later as neurosis, and she would be dead before she saw 30, but at this age, when she smiled, it was genuine. It was the thing that made it all worthwhile. He later realized, when he was married, he would tolerate a lot in exchange for a tiny bit of genuine female happiness. It was a rare commodity.

A few minutes on the road revealed the first problem and it wasn't Laura's bladder; it was the tarp. The tarp was huge and had a lot of slack. When he passed a certain speed, the tarp started to thump and whine and make a terrifying noise.

"Holy shit, we aren't going to hear that the whole time, are we?" she yelled over the noise.

He pulled over and tucked more of the tarp under the boxes and tried to secure the noisy flapping excess. Back in the truck, the adjustments helped, but as they clocked off the first 30 minutes of the trip, he could see the giant surfboard was working loose. There was another stop as he tried various ways to secure it.

Finally, the board was secure enough to forget and the tarp thumping reduced to a low background throb.

So, Laura went to sleep. He nudged her and said "Hey, you can't sleep yet! You have to stay up with me like we agreed."

But she turned her head away and took a deep breath. She slept through the edge of the Valley and slumbered as they passed the big interchange with I-10 in downtown Los Angeles.

He looked up at the Bonaventure Hotel and asked himself again exactly why he was leaving California. The idea had been to take a trip, go home for a while, and then return with a different car, one he could afford. But as the skyscrapers of downtown LA cast their shadow over Laura, he felt a cold fear grip him. It was a long drive, and he knew what was at home; nothing. Comfort and stagnation, or exactly what he had left years earlier. Why was he moving yet again? He did not know and wouldn't know. LA had been his home for years, yet it was somehow, still foreign.

After a few more miles, he was forced to concentrate on the traffic in Rancho Cucamonga and he forgot about his fear for a while.

She woke near sundown.

"I have to pee," she said as she rolled her window down. As she lit a cigarette, she saw the exit signs.

"Redlands? That's as far as we've gone?" she said.

He was glad she was awake, but that meant menthol cigarette smoke in the cab of the truck and multiple stops to pee. When they stopped, he'd have a chance to re-work the tarp, which was starting to make noise again.

At her next pee stop, he moved things around and tried to pull the tarp tighter, but he had underestimated the power of the wind. And, as they moved further out of town and into the high desert on the way to Palm Springs, there were strong crosswinds, and that made new problems.

On top of the rattling tarp sat Gary's surfboard. It was held on with rope that was looped around the big fin and then circled around the nose of the board and then disappeared in the tangle of ropes that were supposed to hold down the tarp. Every time he stopped and re-packed everything, he tried a new combination of loops to secure the board. None made for a silent trip. The ropes hummed and the tarp flapped violently as they sped east and passed through Blythe. The sun set on California behind them.

The hot desert wind didn't cool at all as they reached the night. They passed through Palm Springs and then on to the moonscape of eastern California. There was no truck traffic, and at times, all they could see was a pie shape of light on the highway in front of them.

After she had rested, she smoked and laughed a lot. She could talk, and she modulated her voice up and down in funny ways. She had developed a whole persona of herself as a spoiled brat and would play on that for laughs. She would make fun of herself and that was charming. He laughed a lot at her, and she seemed to like that more than anything else. She was marginally interested in sex and had a fuzzy view of the future, but she was 'good in a room,' as he would later learn the term in Hollywood. She could hold attention. No one had a lukewarm opinion of her.

They reached Phoenix at midnight, and he drove around looking for a Denny's. It was her favorite place to eat, and her selection of favored foods was extremely narrow. They ate and then got back on the road. She fell asleep immediately. At 4:00 AM, be pulled over in Tucson and found a hotel.

In the dark, he unloaded all the boxes and the surfboard and carried them to their room. He was moving quickly because he wanted to get to sleep before sunrise. He knew from bartending about the psychological sleep barrier of seeing the sun come up, so he moved everything out of the truck and into the room as fast as he could, and then climbed into bed with her.

But by mid-morning, she was up and so he was up shortly afterward. She was in a foul mood, and he was resentful that he has to repack the truck alone. The tarp was now partially shredded by the wind and nearly impossible to use. He roped everything in yet a new way and secured the surfboard again and they headed east.

Most of the day, she read and was quiet. He struggled to stay awake and decided that they would stop earlier, sleep through the next night and then continue in the day. Night travel was not going to work, and her legs weren't swelling in the heat anyway.

New Mexico passed by quickly, and she took some photos of the landscapes they encountered. They stopped for gas in Las Cruces, and she took a long time in the bathroom. The thrill of the cross-country trip had worn off and now she was surly most of the time and laughed very little. They blew through El Paso and hit the edge of West Texas at sundown.

"This is the exile," he told her. "From here to San Antonio, you've never seen more nothing."

By early evening, Nick was exhausted. The road was a narrow cone of light in front of them, and he imagined for a while that the truck was sitting still and the road was whirling past under them. It was time to sleep.

They stopped at a motel in Fort Stockton. There was no Denny's, so she ate at McDonald's. They didn't speak at all as he unloaded the truck and lined the boxes along the wall of their tiny room.

He slept well, however. She didn't move or get up early. His was a deep, dreamless sleep.

When he woke, he loaded the truck and he noted the pleasant chill in the desert air. She showered, and they headed out with the sun still low in the east.

The tarp barely covered any of his belongings. His nylon ropes were starting to fray as well, which meant the useful part of the ropes was shorter. A thousand miles of desert travel had worn away his poorly made packing plans, and now he hoped for dry weather all the way to Florida, and he started to short the surfboard to dedicate more rope to holding down what remained of his tarp. The more it flapped about, the less of it he had to work with.

At least she was in a good mood again. She had slept well, and the blasted West Texas landscape held her attention and she took a great many pictures. She was a decent amateur photographer. She saw herself as an artist and would occasionally frame things in an unusual and thoughtful way. Mostly, she just took a lot of better-than-average photos of what was happening around her, which, by itself, was interesting.

A few miles past Fort Stockton, he was watching her fiddle with the settings on her camera and so he didn't see the upcoming dip in the road. Infrequent rains sometimes created riverbeds in the desert and the highway simply plowed right through them. They were well marked, but he didn't see the warning signs and so passed over the edge of the dip at top speed.

The truck lifted heavily and the wheels nearly left the ground. At the moment that the speeding truck shifted from an upward draft to a downward draft and was coming back down on its suspension, the boxes he had recently packed shifted in mid-air and landed in a different configuration.

She made a couple of cracks about him getting her killed while he craned his neck around to look at the boxes and tarp. After some evaluation, he accelerated as everything seemed to be OK. But, back at top speed, he could hear what was left of the tarp flapping about and making a new beating sound. Something had moved and he needed to repack yet again.

He pulled over on the side of the highway and re-packed while she smoked a menthol cigarette. Trucks passed, and he felt the vacuum pulling him into the road. She snapped several photos as he struggled with the ropes and swore at the godforsaken surfboard which took up a lot of rope. He shoved the surfboard further forward to where the nose of the board could be seen from inside the truck. After more swearing from him and laughing from her, they started moving again.

While he had given in to the prospect of day travel with her, he struggled to give in to everything being with her meant. She was going to complain no matter what, and while her whining about food and the constant need to stop annoyed him, somewhere in his mind he knew he had to recognize that he was free to travel this long road, as well as any other, by himself if he wanted and if he wanted her with him, he had to do things a little bit her way. In most ways, he got his way; the truck was his, the town they were going to was his, he was driving, and they were carting all of his stuff. She had the right to an opinion about something.

So, he relaxed a bit, and she smiled. She made him as happy as he was capable of being, which he had realized was not much. She was immature and irascible and many things he needed from her, given that she was the dominant female in his life, he knew he would not get. But, he loved her, and that was something, he thought, he could do nothing about.

"I can't help who I love," he had told Gary just before leaving Los Angeles. Gary shrugged when he said this. It seemed logical but pointless.

As the sun rose higher in the sky, something caught his eye, and he glanced to the left. The shadow of the truck wasn't right. Something was sticking up from the cab of the truck. Then he looked forward and noticed he could no longer see the tip of the surfboard protruding over the front of the truck. He was looking at the shadow of the board which had lifted like a missile about to launch.

"Shit!" he blurted out as he took his foot off the accelerator and moved sharply right to get out of the road.

This was a mistake. The lurch to the right loosened the last connection of the surfboard to the truck and so it lifted off and tumbled backward. Nick watched in the side mirror as the surfboard hit the road, and at some point, he registered the semi coming up in the left lane behind him.

The board hit the highway and bounced. It reached bumper level to the big tractor-trailer and then the truck smashed into the board. The board flew in a wild arc and came to rest in the sand on the right side of the road.

"Goddamit!" Nick said as he brought the truck to a stop.

"What happened?" she asked as she looked around.

"The surfboard flew off," he said as he opened the door and stepped out.

The board, he discovered, was not as damaged as he had anticipated. It had scrapes and dents, but nothing that penetrated the fiberglass casing that wrapped around the foam core. He knelt and turned it over and over, inspecting the damage.

He noted that the fin had snapped off, but he also thought this wasn't a problem because the fin was a modular piece and he could replace it. But, when he put the board back on the top of the truck and tried to tie it back on, he realized tying it down was now impossible. The fin was the only handle the board had. Less the fin, there was nothing else to tie onto.

He realized this not in a single moment but as part of an ever more irritating process as he tried different combinations to secure the board. He was becoming more agitated as the inevitable conclusion closed in on him. The board was lost not because it was damaged, but because now there was no way to secure it.

He began to swear more and clench his fists in frustration. He tried to wrap the board around the middle and squeeze it into place, but his tie-down ability with the frayed, cheap rope wouldn't allow for enough pressure. He thought of somehow punching a hole in the board so it could be secured, but he didn't have the tools for such a thing and was sure the board would be ruined if he snapped it in half.

Mercifully, she stood on the side of the road, smoked a cigarette, and watched in silence. After a while, she stubbed the cigarette out with her boot and spoke.

"You have to let this go," she said. She wasn't kidding, she wasn't being funny, and there was a never-before-heard sound of compassion in her voice. He stopped what he was doing and looked at her.

"There's nothing you can do, and it isn't your fault," she said. When she didn't follow that statement up with a zinger or an insult, he looked down at the dusty ground.

"Let it go," she said, simply. "You've done all you can. Some things just won't work."

He lifted the board off the truck and walked several yards off the road. Then he lifted the surfboard, a device made for riding ocean waves and threw it into the desert. They had come as far away from an ocean as I-10 allowed for, at the mid-point between Santa Monica and Jacksonville, and here, he was leaving a surfboard. It made about as much sense as the whole trip.

He got back in the truck and smiled. It was funny, really. She laughed and snapped a photo of him.

It started to rain when they reached Louisiana, but the boxes and the remaining tarp protected his things for the most part. After four days and part of the night, they reached his parents' home.

She acted like she hated Florida and wasn't friendly to his family. She made a terrible impression on all she met, and after a month, she flew home to California. Before he returned to California to try again with her, she went back to Gary.

I-10

———

Rusty tried to like the people he worked with, but it was hard.

He learned how to make money selling used cars from a neighbor when he was a teen, and it was a good business. When he opened a used car lot and started selling cars full time, he had to hire a sales staff to stay at the lot while he was out looking for cars. After a few years, he had hired, fired, or lost a rolling series of salespeople, and he hated them all. They were the living, breathing cliché used car salesmen everyone knew and now he was the king of these stupid, fat motherfuckers.

Still, he had to have them. He couldn't do it all himself, and he had to stay involved so they wouldn't steal from him which meant he had to drop by every day which meant he had to deal with all their bullshit.

He hired several female sellers and invested a lot of training time in them and it had worked out great for a while. Good-looking females could move the iron, but they would quit after a few weeks without fail. The men at the lot would talk to them non-stop, or a customer would start to stalk them, or they would just find a nicer place to work, and move on. When the girls would quit, the older guys would smirk and sit down more.

He upgraded the office but that was mostly for him. Upgrades didn't keep the female sellers around as he had hoped, customers didn't seem to care, and the salesmen laughed at the colors he chose. They thought he should just pay them more. Fine, he thought. Further upgrades were contained to his office only, which was made very nice. His office had rugs and art. The rest of the office had wood paneling.

Eventually, he took the cappuccino machine home and resigned himself to the routine of the business; he came in first thing in the morning to make sure they were open and everyone showed up, and he came by in the late afternoon to proof paperwork and collect cash and checks. The middle of the day was his.

When sales were slow, he'd fire the weakest sellers and handle some of the work himself, but mostly he stayed away. His system had been honed over the years through trial and error, and now the business spun off cash without much input from him. He bought cars at the auctions and ran an entire secondary business selling performance and luxury automobiles on his own. He kept the luxury cars at his house and did the paperwork himself at home.

The one time he liked to be on the lot was when he had to shoot a new TV commercial. He liked to see himself on TV. His cable sales person was a good-looking woman and he liked her. He genuinely felt she was not trying to screw him over, but he still kept his contracts and checked his invoices. Once, he found a discrepancy and waited for her to come by to sell him something new and then confronted her about it. He could tell by the look on her face that she was aghast at the accusation that she had tried to deceive him. When she blushed and started to cry, he got angry and told her to leave.

That afternoon, he sent her flowers. She called him the next day, and when he told her he had never sent flowers to anyone, she said something that summed up what he had been feeling but hadn't able to articulate: "You're finding out new things about yourself," she said.

Those words made him feel great. Later that day, he booked a massage for himself since he had never done that either. It was heavenly.

He was driving to Biloxi to look at a Porsche when he called in to the lot to check on things. His fattest salesman said, "You got a call from a nurse about your grandfather." Rusty snapped back, "My grandfather is dead." The fattest salesperson didn't ask any questions and moved on. But later, as Rusty was nearing the exits off the 10 to Biloxi, he called back and asked for more details.

"She was calling from that old folk's home up by the university," the fat guy said. "She said your grandfather had seen you on TV and wanted to talk to you. She said he was sick, and if you were interested, you should call."

"Text me the phone number," Rusty said and hung up. A few minutes later, the phone number arrived.

The Porsche in Biloxi was very clean and well-priced. Still, Rusty shook his head, and looked disappointed. "This car needs a lot of work," he said as he walked around it. The owner leaned on his cane. Rusty kept shaking his head. He got the man to come down 25% on the price and they made the deal.

On his way home, he called the number. As it was ringing, he started to get anxious. When a woman answered the phone, he hung up. For a few miles, he asked himself why he hung up, and why he had called in the first place. When he had satisfied himself with the answers to those questions, he dialed the number again.

"This is Rusty Grimes. I got a call from your," he paused, unsure what to call it, "facility about my grandfather," he said. He liked to put his name out there because often, people knew him because they had bought a car from him or seen him on TV.

"What's his name?" the nurse asked. Rusty caught his breath. He didn't want to say the name.

"Probably, it's Willie Moye," he said.

"Hold on," the nurse said.

He fought the urge to hang up again as he waited. Finally, another nurse picked up the line.

"Mr. Grimes! Good to talk to you. This is Nurse Tina," she said. She sounded young and happy, and she had a light Latin accent.

"Yeah, hey, you're the one that called?" he asked.

"Yes, it was me!" she said. Goddamn, she sounded happy. "I met you before. I bought my car from you and I love it!'

Now Rusty was warming to her. "What kind of car did you buy?"

"It's a Camero and I love it. A Camero was my dream car. I always wanted one since I was a little girl. My Papa drove one, and you found me one that's red just like I wanted," she said.

"Well, I'm glad I could find it for you," he said, slipping into sales mode. "Those are hot cars, and the people who drive them really love them."

"Well, I love mine," she said warmly. "You know, we've had a gentleman here for a couple of years and he just told me the other day that he was your grandfather. He sees you on TV all the time and he finally told me that you were his grandson."

"Well, he might not have told you that we aren't close, and we haven't seen each other in a long time," he said, trying not to sound angry, which he was.

"I suspected you two were estranged," she said. He liked the way she said 'estranged' in her accent.

"Yes, we're very estranged," Rusty said. "My dad is dead, he died in prison, and that old man is responsible."

He regretted what he said as soon as he said it. It wasn't technically true, which he knew. His dad was let out before he died, and Willie went to jail for the same crime and he could have pled out and testified against Rusty's dad, but he didn't. Still, Rusty blamed him. He was the older one and he should have known better. The man was a shit father and a shit father-in-law and a miserable fuck stick and Rusty never had much use for him after his dad went to prison.

"I understand," Nurse Tina said. "Well, he wanted to me ask you if you'd come to visit him, and that's all I'm doing. He's not well, and he can't talk much, but he's aware and he wants to see you."

Rusty started to speak, but then decided not to. Instead, he hung up. A few minutes later, he called back.

"I'm sorry I hung up on you," he said to Nurse Tina. "That was rude. Please don't tell the old man anything. I'll come by if I can."

She was nice about it. Whoever she was, he decided, she was going to get flowers.

The days clocked by quickly. He was in a groove and the cars sailed off his lot.

He attended the auctions and bought more cars. The sellers and wholesalers all knew and liked him. They knew he could move cars. He knew when to stop negotiating and just close the deal. Because he knew when to stop trying to get a lower price, the wholesalers and other car sources would tip him first when they had something special, like a good used Honda, so he got cars no one else had and he sold them faster and for more money. He may have hated all the fat slobs that worked for him, but those jackasses could sell cars. They could keep his machine moving.

That afternoon, he arrived to check paper work and pick up checks. He paused for a moment, and just watched to see what his staff was doing. They were all inside sitting down and doing nothing. It occurred to him that he had never, not once, had a good sales person who went out on his own and opened a competitive car lot. They knew cars, they knew what he did, but they wouldn't do it themselves. They wouldn't step out of the safety of working for someone else. Any of his sales staff would be better prepared to start a used car lot than he had been when he first started out. His first lot was 2000 square feet and he had six cars. He had used his car for an office back then.

After a moment, he went inside, took care of business and left.

Christmas passed and he thought about his grandfather. He sent flowers to Nurse Tina after they had spoken and he sent more for Christmas. By mid-January, he had run through all the possible dialogue that might occur between himself and Willie Moye. In this way, he had talked himself into seeing the old man. Plus, there were a couple of factual questions he wanted answered and he knew Willie could answer them.

"Mr. Grimes, thank you so much for the flowers! They are just beautiful and it was so nice of you to send them!" Nurse Tina said. On the phone, she sounded as cheery as ever.

"You're welcome," he said nervously. He didn't do well with thanks or praise unless it was about cars.

"They were just beautiful and I really appreciate it," she said.

"So, uh," he stammered. He couldn't get the words out.

"Your grandfather is fine," she said without him needing to ask. She was clearly an empath. "There hasn't been much change with him. He likes to watch those crime shows, like the ones with cold cases. And he still points you out on the TV to everyone."

"If I wanted to talk to him, in private, how might I do that?" he asked nervously.

"All you have to do is show up," she said.

He had sort of hoped there was something else to it, something that would prevent him from going. But there wasn't. If he went, he'd get to talk to the old man.

After a few more weeks, he picked a date in his mind to go. He decided on a Wednesday when car sales were typically slow. He stopped by the lot that morning, looking for something that might occupy the whole day and not finding that, he went to the facility where his grandfather lay.

As soon as he entered, a nurse with very black hair smiled at him. That is Nurse Tina, he thought.

"I know that face!" she said. She was clearly Latin. She had flat, straight, black hair and olive skin. She was petite, with a rounded shape from her arms to her legs to her torso. She had a fine face with nice features and a robust smile. She had a long Spanish nose that came to a point. It was the only sharp feature she possessed.

"It's me," he said softly.

They chatted for a moment and then she came around the desk and slid her arms into his like they were walking down a wedding aisle.

"He's going to be so happy to see you!" she said.

It didn't take long to reach Willie. Rusty was just starting to absorb all the aged, sickly, drugged people around him when she stopped, and he realized he was standing in front of an old man lying on a wheeled hospital bed that was positioned in front of a TV. The old man had already seen him. Nurse Tina let go of his arm and he found himself caught in the gaze of Willie Moye.

Willie had all his hair and it was a comely mix of white and iron gray. Below that, a sun burned and age-spotted forehead wrinkled over two thick white eye brows that shielded two deep blue eyes.

Willie's eyes had been the subject of many conversations. Some had been between admiring females and some between witnesses and law enforcement. Willie had fabulous blue eyes and he knew it and he had traded on them his whole life. When Rusty looked at them, his first thought was that those goddamn eyes had bought his grandfather the affection of Nurse Tina. They were that good, and he still had them.

Nurse Tina slid a chair up behind him and before he could say anything further, she left without a word. Suddenly, Rusty was sitting and those amazing blue eyes were staring down on him. It was a perspective that he immediately remembered and it paralyzed him in place.

Willie said something and then motioned for Rusty to move closer. Rusty leaned in and scooted his chair closer. Willie spoke as loud as he could. He voice was a raspy whisper.

"I can't talk very loud," he said.

"That's OK," Rusty said.

"I know you won't stay long. You look good. You're making money," Willie said. His eyes nearly disappeared behind a crinkly smile.

"How can you tell?" Rusty asked.

"You've put on weight. You're wearing nice shoes. You smell like a girl. You've got a fucking silver ring on your right hand. You're rich," he said.

Rusty felt a rich vein of emotions surge through him but he looked down. One of those emotions was pride.

"What kind of car you drive here?" Willie asked.

"It's a Porsche Boxster. I'm trying to sell it," he said.

Willie closed his eyes tight in triumph. His hand came out from under the sheet and he gave Rusty huge thumbs up.

"I'm so proud of you," he whispered.

Rusty had no idea that this was going to happen. He just stared at his shoes. He didn't know he would become a little boy again in Willie's presence.

"Hey, I got something I want to tell you about," Willie said. He reached over to the rolling stand beside him and picked up a Bible. He opened it and took out a folded piece of paper. He carefully unfolded the paper and held it up.

"I drew this a long time ago. In 1975, I paid a guy to rob a bank in Santa Fe. He got some money, we split it up, and then I bought some drugs and brought them back from Mexico. I sold those, but they caught the guy that robbed the bank so I needed to get rid of the money," he said.

Rusty felt a rising tide of anger. He had been confronted with various kinds of bad guys in his life as a car dealer. Once, he caught a guy on his lot trying to break into a car. He tackled the guy and took his wallet as the guy fled. It turned out to be a 17-year-old who lived next door. He caught homeless guys sleeping in his cars and he caught one of his sales people selling speed during work hours. He had been in many confrontations with unhappy customers. He wasn't fearful, but he tried to forget that his dad and grandfather were real criminals and they did big time crimes. They carried guns and had fights with the cops and other gangsters. They had surely killed people. That life is how they drew huge sentences and spent significant time in jail. The man before him was the original outlaw. He had coached Rusty's dad into the life.

"I just came to say hello, not talk about stuff from the past," Rusty said.

Willie smiled.

"I know, but I don't have much time," he said. "You need to take this with you."

He handed the piece of paper to Rusty.

"In 1979, I had a friend that ran a gas station outside Las Cruces. That's in New Mexico right off the 10. I buried a lot of money and other stuff behind that station. I have no idea what happened to him, or that station, but I buried it deep, and the guy that owned the station didn't know where. Only I knew. But I never went back. I think it's still there. Go get it, and it's yours," said Willy as he passed the paper from his shaking hands to Rusty.

Rusty looked at paper. It was a hand-drawn map of intersecting roads with an X where the station sat. Interstate 10 was marked as well. He flipped the note over. On the back was a crude drawing of the gas station and an X off the back corner of the building. The number four was written beside the X.

"You buried some money in 1979 and you think it's still there?" Rusty said sarcastically.

"I looked at a picture of the area on the computer," he said. "There's nothing there except the concrete slab of the station. I can see right where I put it. No one has touched that earth. It's there."

"What makes you think I want it?" Rusty said. "I have over a million dollars in the bank. It's all in my checking account."

"Ha! That's bullshit," Willie said.

Rusty snapped out of his trance and stood.

"No, it isn't, but this is a bullshit story," he said. "I have some questions for you though."

"Shoot," said Willie. Somehow, he was still smiling.

"Did you come up with the idea to rob the bank when my dad was arrested?" Rusty asked. He was starting to hyperventilate.

Willie took a deep breath and looked at the TV screen. He stopped smiling and closed his eyes.

"No. That was his idea. I told him banks were too well-defended at that point," Willie said. "He had someone inside that he was working with, but he was on drugs; coke mostly. That shit makes you into an idiot."

Willie paused and took a deep breath.

"God, I miss that boy," Willie said. "He was the greatest kid in the world."

"What happened at the trial?"Rusty asked.

"I told them it was all my idea but they knew it wasn't. They had video. His inside guy had turned on him. I was convicted of perjury trying to help him. It's public record, Russ," Willie said.

"How did he die?" Rusty asked.

"He had cancer!" Willie said as loud as he could. "They let him out because he was so sick and he died in the hospital. I was still in but he got out and then he died. Your mother told you all kinds of things, but they weren't true. I didn't kill him!"

Rusty turned and walked towards the exits. He saw Nurse Tina out of the corner of his eye but he didn't speak. He started running once he reached the parking lot and he felt a little safer when he was in the Porsche and it was locked. That's when he noticed that he still had Willie's tiny map in his hand.

He dropped the map on the floor board and fired up the Porsche. He revved the engine, hoping that Willie would hear it, and then he peeled out of the lot, leaving a rubber streak behind.

Another few weeks passed and he sold many more cars. When he had an offer for the Boxster, he took the map inside and put it in the office safe. He tried not to think about it, but that was not so easy. On several occasions, he took the map out and looked at it. Then, he did what he had told himself he would not do; he tried to find the location himself with Google maps.

The gas station had been on a corner and so the intersection was not hard to find. Willie had the highway names correct. He zoomed in and looked at the spot that was marked on Willie's map. It was there, and it showed no signs of being disturbed. The closest building looked to be a truck stop about 1000 yards away.

A few days later, his wine club shipment arrived. He saw the case sitting on the porch as he pulled up the drive way in the Lexus he had bought from an estate sale earlier that day. In the case was a Pinot Nior. He thought it was a bit watery. He liked the flavor of Pinots, but they were teasing him, he felt, and he would rather cavort with a sturdy, straightforward cabernet. After he downed a couple of glasses of the Pinot just to be sure, he scooped up the case and put it in the empty trunk of the Lexus.

Nurse Tina was there by herself when he arrived. He set the case of Pinot on the reception counter.

"Mr. Grimes! How nice to see you!" she said enthusiastically.

"Good to see you. Do you like Pinots?" he said.

She looked at the case.

"Pinot Nior or Pinot Grigio?" she asked.

"Nior," he said. "I have a whole case but I don't like it much. You can have it if you enjoy it."

She started to say something but then didn't. After a beat, she smiled broadly.

"That is so nice of you! Yes, I'd love to have it. Can I share it with the staff here?" she asked.

"You can do whatever you like with it, as long as you enjoy it. I want someone to like it," he said as he realized his voice was shaking. "Is Willie awake?"

"I don't know, but let's go see," she said.

This time, she didn't take his arm, but she led him to Willie's bed, which hadn't moved from where it was. Willie was asleep, but she gently shook his arm.

"Mr. Moye, your grandson is here to see you," she said softly. As Willie came awake, Rusty looked around the room. Most of the elderly were slumped over in wheelchairs or lying down. Their faces were contorted in pain or blank like the dead. He wondered how he hadn't noticed the morbid horror of the place the last time he had been there.

Suddenly, Nurse Tina was gone and Rusty was staring at Willie. Willie wasn't smiling, and appeared to be in pain. Rusty sat and leaned in close.

"The X on the map: are you sure it's in the right place?" he said.

"It's four feet from the corner. The joint where the sidewalk turns points to it, and its exactly four feet from the edge of the concrete," Willie said.

"What is it? A bag? A box? What am I looking for?" he said.

"It's a suitcase," Willie whispered. "A big, cheap suitcase made out of plastic. But I put everything in other plastic bags and boxes and stuff, so it should have stayed dry."

"How big?" Rusty asked.

Willie lifted his hands and spread them far apart.

"How far down?" Rusty asked.

"Pretty far. I got down in the hole and dug and it was up to my waist at least," he said.

"Did anyone else know? Anyone else might have already dug it up?" Rusty asked.

"Your dad knew. He was with me. But he never went there."

Rusty hung his head. They were both there.

"What's in it? How much money?" Rusty asked.

"I don't remember, but it's at least couple hundred thousand."

"That's all? You know, I make that much every few months, and I don't have to hide it," Rusty said. It agitated him that they had made such messes of their lives for so little.

"That was a lot of money then," Willie said. "There's some other stuff. Your dad liked to buy gold rings and stuff to wear or give away to women. It was gaudy shit I told him attracted attention, but he liked it. And there are some pictures and some other stuff. We were trying to get rid of anything that would connect us to that guy in Santa Fe, but we put other things we thought we might want in there, too."

Willie closed his eyes. Rusty could tell he was way back in time.

"If I get it, what do you want me to do with it?" Rusty asked.

"Keep it! Enjoy it. It won't do me any good. Give it away if you want," Willy said. "Everything in that suit case took me and your dad years to build up, and I don't want it to just sit there forever."

Willie turned his head away. Now, he was in pain.

"I might go," Rusty said. "I'm a legit business person and I don't want to get involved in you and my dad's dead bullshit. I never did. But now I'm curious and I know I'll probably do this sooner or later. But I'm not promising anything."

"Do what the hell you want. I'm dead soon," Willie whispered. "And I'm sorry about your dad, but you didn't love him like I did. He and I were best friends. You never had a dad and I'm sorry. I told him he should go get you. But I did have a son, and I lost him. I've not been able to be happy or like anything about life since then. I'm ready to move on."

The next thing Rusty knew he was in his car and huge tears were running down his face. When he got home, he pulled another bottle of wine down from his rack, this time a cabernet, and he had a big glass before going to bed.

The next morning, he was at the lot at sunrise. He walked around the looking at trucks. He had quite a few, including a Ram that was super clean. It was jet black and low mileage. He remembered buying it and was surprised it was still there.

He opened the safe behind his desk and took out $2000 in cash and Willie's map while his computer booted up. He couldn't resist the urge to look at the spot online again. He zoomed in on the footprint of the gas station. Willie's map was beside the screen as he zoomed in on the portion that Willie had marked with a faded red X.

A car pulled up and he heard a door shut. It wasn't quite 6:30 yet, he thought, way too early for the fat fingered dummies he hired. The front door opened and Ted, one of his sales guys, came in.

"Good morning!" he called out to Rusty.

"You're here early," Rusty said.

"Yeah, I got some more paper work to do on what we sold yesterday. Man, we were jumping! Twelve cars in a day might be a record, right?" he said cheerily.

Rusty realized then that he hadn't done anything that he normally did in the morning, which included checking the lock box for contracts. He hadn't been in the previous night either.

"You guys sold twelve cars yesterday?" he asked.

"Yeah! Twelve nice ones, too! You didn't look in the lock box yet?" Ted inquired.

Rusty stared at Ted as Ted logged on to his computer. He suddenly realized that he didn't hate Ted. Ted was a decent guy, and he had worked there for over 10 years.

"What's your wife doing, Ted?" he asked. "Didn't you say she opened a salon or something?"

Ted looked up. Personal questions were unusual, and now he was on alert.

"Yeah, she opened a nail salon," he said. "All her friends come over and yak and get their nails done and their feet worked on."

"Does it make money?" Rusty asked.

"Yeah," Ted said, "It makes a little money. It's cheap to operate, and as long as she's there to run it, it makes some money. She needs to find some good employees so she can grow, though. She can't find anyone she likes."

He processed the paperwork from the previous day and then locked up his desk and then his office. By the time he was ready to leave, the rest of the staff was there and most were sitting at their desks talking and laughing. Rusty called to Ted and motioned for him to come outside.

"I want you to see if you can sell that Lexus," Rusty said to Ted as he handed him a folder. "Just you. Anyone wants to drive it, you go with them. We'll take 22, so mark it at 28. I'll give you 15 percent if you can sell it."

Ted took the folder, but his brow was furrowed. This was not the Rusty he was used to and he was worried.

"I'm taking the black Ram truck for a couple of days," he said. "Don't put anything in the lock box until I get back. Take it home with you and keep it somewhere safe."

"OK," Ted said. "Everything alright?"

"Yeah, I just need to take a break," Rusty said. "Don't let things get fucked up around here."

When he got home, he smelled bleach, so he knew the cleaning lady must have come that morning. He barely touched anything in the house and he cleaned up after himself anyway, so he didn't really need a cleaning lady, but she folded his laundry and dusted the baseboards and he liked that.

As he opened a new bottle of cabernet, he thought about Christmas that had past recently. He had never decorated his house for Christmas or bought a Christmas tree. He poured himself another glass of cabernet and bought some Christmas songs on his phone and then connected the phone to his stereo. He sat down on the coffee table and listened. The Christmas songs echoed through the big, empty house.

"Have yourself a merry little Christmas," he sang along, but he didn't know the other words so he just listened.

That night, he went to an expensive restaurant and sat at the bar. He tried some new appetizers, but they were too salty. As he waited on his entrée, he ran his plans through his head over and over. When his food arrived, he decided to stop thinking about the map and his plan. He had a very good glass of Grenache and listened to the sounds of people around him, then went home and went to sleep.

By sunrise, he was in western Louisiana. The elevated portion of I-10 took him over miles of swamp land. Steam rose off the dark waters below. His phone was turned off and he rode in silence. He thought about the trip along I-10 he had taken with his dad.

He was living with his mother in Jacksonville and his dad had just shown up one day. Rusty saw him down the block from his house. His dad told him to get in the car. He had clothes and a plan.

"We're going to California!" he announced as they pulled away.

Rusty didn't want to go; he was afraid of his dad, and he knew his mom wouldn't ever let him go but his dad got on I-10 and headed west. When they got to Mobile, Alabama, he convinced his dad to call his mom and tell her where he was.

His dad called his mother collect on a pay phone and said "Russ is with me, we're fine, and we're just taking a little trip." Then he hung up.

They drove all the way to California on the 10. They ate at McDonald's and slept in the car somewhere in Texas. When they got to California, his dad showed him off to his friends like he was a prize. It made him feel good at first, but he could tell his dad's friends didn't care about some kid. A couple of times, his dad left him with friends and disappeared for a day. Rusty was very scared then. One of his dad's friends made him sit outside all day long. But his dad always came back.

After five weeks, his mother tracked them down and came and got him. He flew on an airplane for the first time on the way back to Florida. His dad was in jail the next time he saw him and then he was dead.

They drove right past the buried suitcase, he thought, and it was there when his dad tried to rob that final bank. Why didn't he just go dig it up himself?

The South gave way to the West just outside of San Antonio. The landscape grew more barren and dry so he rolled his window down. The cool air felt great. His thoughts were sharp as a pin. He had been on the road for 12 hours already, but he was wide awake. His timing was going to be close. He would arrive in Las Cruces at sundown.

West Texas was as he remembered. It was not only vast; it was hypnotic. He and his dad had stopped somewhere in the area to sleep and he recalled waking in the middle of the night and getting out of the car to pee. The place was another planet. Stars filled the sky and lit up the night, and he could see the arc of the Milky Way reaching up from the horizon with his own eyes. It was summer then and while the nights were cool, the days had been very hot. Now, it was winter. He rolled down both windows and let the cool, dry air blast through the cab of the truck.

The sun was low on the horizon when he passed through El Paso. Just past the city, the 10 ran parallel to the Rio Grande. To his right, he saw lines of street lights going up in the hills. To his left he saw darkness descending on the pueblo buildings of Mexico. For a moment, he thought about Nurse Tina. Was she from Mexico? How did she end up with such a sunny attitude?

At sundown, he reached Las Cruces. He knew the exit he needed to take. The twinkling lights of the town sparkled in the distance as he exited I-10 and drove along a frontage road for a few miles. He saw the truck stop up ahead. The sky was a deep red behind it. He slowed down and looked for the road that would mark the intersection where the gas station once stood.

Suddenly, he braked hard. In the twilight, he had missed the intersection. A car was coming up from behind, so he pulled over, let that car pass, and then turned around.

He rolled through the intersection and on to the lot where the gas station had once stood. When he reached the old dirty cement slab, he stopped the truck and turned everything off. The hot truck pinged in the cool air as his eyes adjusted to the dark.

He got out of the truck and walked towards the slab. Behind him, he could see the truck stop. A big rig was pulling out. That rig would pass soon, but that would be OK. The trucker would be out of state in a short time and he wouldn't care or remember a man standing on an old slab on the side of the road at sunset.

The station had been small. The walls had been made of concrete block and the outlines of the walls were evident. Here had been a door, there had been a small hallway, over there was the double service bay. Closer to the road he could see the concrete rectangle that marked where the pumps had been.

The station had a sidewalk that led to the bathrooms in the back. He could see the tile floors where the bathrooms had been. The holes that marked where the plumbing had been were still visible. He crossed through one of the bathrooms and then came to the corner of the building.

Where the slab stopped and the sidewalk started was hard to tell. Everything had dirt on it. He noticed that a line of weeds stood where the crumbled wall had collected enough dirt for them to grow. From the weed line, he used the toe of his boot to scrape away the soil that revealed the sidewalk. It was there. He kneeled down and used his hand to brush away the dirt until he found the diagonal seam in the concrete that marked where it turned to go around the back of the building. He traced his finger in that seam until he reached its end. He dug his finger along the rim of the concrete to the left and then back to the right until he had created an arrow.

He took a tape measure off his belt. From the arrow he had dug, he pulled the tape measure out four feet. In the last of the light, he stuck his finger in the dirt beside the four then he reached in to his pocket and took out a glow stick he had bought the day before at a party store. He stuck the glow stick in the dirt and stood. This was the spot. If there was anything down there, it was right below him. The big rig rumbled past as he climbed back in his truck.

He kept his windows down as he drove around Las Cruces looking for the best restaurant. After driving around for a while, he settled on the Cattle Baron Steak and Seafood Grill. He took a seat at the deep mahogany-colored bar and looked around. He was pleased. The interior was dark wood with low yellow lights all around. The bartender recommended a California red; it was wonderful. It had a smoky flavor he liked and an after taste of chocolate. He ordered a bottle of the red and a steak with seared vegetables. He ate slowly and let each bite stay in his mouth a long time. Everything tasted so wonderful. He finished most of the bottle and had a desert of what they called chocolate lava cake. It was chocolate cake with a thick, dark chocolate sauce drizzled over it. A rich red strawberry was positioned on top.

He left a big tip and then moved his truck around to the back of the restaurant and got in the back seat and lay down. He had brought one of his pillows from home, and it smelled like the fabric softener his housekeeper used. He lay his head on the pillow and fell to sleep immediately.

He woke a couple of times and looked at his watch in the dark. It was still too early. He drifted back to sleep. At 1:30, he woke and decided it was late enough. He climbed into the front seat and rolled the windows down and drove away.

The desert was black. As he neared the intersection, he could see the glow of lights on I-10 but the sky was overcast so there was no moon. He drove past the intersection and turned into the truck stop.

He went inside and looked around. It was a big truck plaza with aisles full of food, clothes, hats, all kinds of drinks, and lots of key chains. He looked at the wines they had for sale and wrinkled his nose; it was all shit. He bought a cup of faux French roast coffee and then pumped his gas. A few cars came and went, and he lingered around, trying to time the average traffic flows and observe which direction traffic came from. There was no pattern. Cars had to pass the intersection where the old station had stood to get back to the 10. No matter how fast he dug, he would be there digging as cars and trucks passed.

He drove to the dark intersection. As soon as his headlights picked up the slab, he turned them off then stopped the truck between where he would dig and the road. He opened the glove box and took out a handful of glow sticks. He bent them enough to cause them to ignite.

The green light of the glow sticks was enough for him to find his way to the one glow stick he had placed at sundown. He set the three glow sticks down on the corners of where he wanted to dig then ignited the one he had left and set it on the last corner. Now, there was a glowing square on the ground.

He reached into the bed of the truck and lifted out a shovel and a pick axe. Both still had the bar codes on the handles. He threw the pick axe down and pushed the shovel nose into the dirt at the center of the glowing square.

A few minutes later, he had to move his glow sticks back as the hole grew. The dirt was getting harder so he threw the shovel down and lifted the pick axe and started chopping. After swinging the pick axe a few times, he stopped to catch his breath. He was sweating and this was making him cold. He took a black jacket from the seat of the truck, pulled it on, and then picked up the shovel again.

His mind raced. He thought about Nurse Tina and Willie. He imagined his dad and Willie digging at the same spot. He wondered how far he should dig before giving up. What if he got down three feet and there was nothing? What about four feet? What if Willie had made up the whole thing? Why didn't his dad stop when they were on the way to California? Or did they, and he didn't remember?

He was getting chilled again, but he was digging faster. He slung dirt as far away as he could and he covered two of his glow sticks. He took a maglite out of his pocket and turned it on long enough to look at the hole. It was deep, and now he had to step in it to go down further.

Under this jacket, he could feel his shirt soaking with sweat. He stopped trying to dig a big hole and concentrated on digging a deep hole. He had gone down at least four feet. The soil was softer and it came up in damp, heavy shovels full.

He counted out twenty five shovels full and then took out his maglite and looked at what he had dug. He was several feet deep and standing in dirt up to his ankles. He stuck the end of the light in his mouth so he could see and threw out ten more big shovels full. He thought about taking a short break, but decided not to. Then he felt the shovel head strike something a tiny bit solid.

He stopped and looked with the maglite. There was nothing. He dug more carefully and scooped out more dirt. Then he felt the shovel head strike something solid again. Not rock solid, but more solid than the dirt.

He dropped down on to one knee and used his hands to scoop away dirt. He felt something with his fingers. He pushed away more dirt. A drop of sweat fell from the end of his nose. He pushed back enough dirt to see a solid piece of blue. He pushed away more dirt. The blue had a slight texture. It had a feel. It was plastic. Then he cleared away more and he found a corner. Then he felt down and could feel the seam. It was a suitcase.

He leaned back and sat down in the hole. It was here. Willie wasn't a liar. He was a thief, a crook, and a bad man, but he wasn't, nor had he ever been, a liar.

He grabbed the shovel and stood. He would be gone in a few minutes.

But then he was staring into two headlights. They were far apart and square, and he knew they were from an older American car, probably a Lincoln Town Car. The driver's side door opened but he couldn't see who got out. Whoever it was, they switched on a flashlight and shown it on his face.

"What you doing here?" he heard a voice say. It was an older man. He lifted his maglite and tried to illuminate the person with the flashlight, but he couldn't make out much.

"What you looking for?" the man asked.

"None of your business," he said, and climbed out of the hole. The man with the light stepped back.

"I'm carrying," he said. "Don't get stupid. This is my lot, and you're digging on it. Answer me. I don't want to call the police."

Rusty thought hard. Was this the station owner? What were the chances? Pretty low he thought.

"I'm just looking for something," he said. "I'm not looking for trouble or stealing anything or hurting anyone. I'll be on my way in a few more minutes. If this is your lot, maybe there are some things you don't know. Give me a few minutes; I'll make it worth your while. I don't want the police either."

A long silence followed. He could hear the man breathing hard and he could see the car was an old Lincoln Town Car.

"You ain't Willie Moye," the voice said. "And I don't think you're his son, neither."

Rusty's mind did some quick math. Willie said no one knew about the suitcase, but whoever this guy was, he had linked digging with Willie. The truth was the best option at this point. Or, at least some portion of it.

"Willie sent me. He's an old man now. He sent me here to claim what's in this hole," Rusty said. "Give me a few minutes, and I'll be gone."

"Who are you?"

"What difference does it make?" Rusty said. "You know Willie and if I'm here digging, I know him, too."

"I want to know. Who are you?" the stranger asked.

Rusty did some more math.

"Willie's grandson. He sent me here," he said.

The man reached inside the car and turned the headlights off. He then walked over and shined his flashlight in the hole. Rusty got a look at him. He was an old man with long gray and black hair. He had on a black jacket with jeans and cowboy boots.

"I didn't think no one was ever coming back," he said.

"You owned the station?" Rusty asked.

"Yeah," the man said. "I own that one over there, too." He nodded at the truck stop. "Did you find it?"

"I think so. I just reached it," Rusty said.

Rusty jumped back in the hole and scooped the dirt back. The old man shown his light down and now they could clearly see the corner of a suitcase.

"Go on," the old man said. "I'll hold the light."

Rusty didn't want to turn his back on the old man. If he knew the case was connected to Willie, he had to know it had money in it. The old man was armed and Rusty was standing in a man-sized hole, but he had little choice, so he heaved more dirt out and dug around the corner of the case. After a few more scoops, he was able to grab the side of the case. After scooping away more dirt with his hands, he was able to move it. Then, he was able to lift it. It was heavy, and slick with moist dirt, but he lifted it up and set it on the ground at the feet of the old man. The old man offered his hand and helped Rusty climb out of the hole.

Rusty lifted the case and set it on the tailgate of the truck. The old man held the light while he brushed and blew dirt out of the two silver latches that held the case closed. Rusty tried to pull them open, but they wouldn't move. He used the shovel blade to wedge in behind one of the latches and it popped open and then he could partially open the case. He was able to work on the other latch until it opened as well and he pushed the case all the way open.

The old man shown his light across bunches of plastic bags. Rusty leaned in and studied them. He touched one, and felt the money inside it. He tore the plastic enough to see the edges of stacks of bills inside.

"You need to go," the old man said.

"I'll give you some. For renting this space from you for all those years," he said.

"No, I don't want nothing. Bad luck. I'm legitimate businessman. I don't need no money. That damn truck stop makes me rich," he said flatly. "You should go. Police, they come by all the time and I don't want no questions and no drugs on my property."

"OK. Thanks for your help," Rusty said and shut the case.

"Tell Willie Popper said hello," the old man said.

Rusty turned on his maglite and shown it briefly at the old man. He saw the ancient face of a pure Navaho Indian with a huge broad nose and thick lips and wood-colored skin.

"Popper. Is that your name?" he asked.

"That's what he called me." Popper said. "Now everyone calls me that. I popped a lot of pills, so Willie called me Popper. It stuck."

"I'll do it," Rusty said. "You knew my dad?" he asked before he could stop himself.

"Yeah," Popper said as he turned back towards his car. "Tell him I said hello, too."

The old man said nothing further. He got in his old Lincoln and left as Rusty wrapped the suitcase in a heavy tarp. He threw the shovel and pick axe in the back of the truck and in less than a minute, he was back on I-10, headed east.

Rusty Grimes drove silently through the rest of the night. He thought of nothing, but he felt very good. Somewhere around Fort Stockton, he put on the Christmas music he had bought. The windows were down and the music was loud. He smiled broadly and deeply.

The sun was rising as he past San Antonio. When he was east of the city, larger trees and greener grasses populated the landscape and the air became humid enough to feel the cold so he rolled the windows up. He pulled over to get gas in Houston, and then pulled around behind the gas station and put the tailgate down. He unwrapped the suitcase and opened it.

There were many bags in the case neatly stacked on top of each other. That was Willie's doing, he thought. Most were filled with money. He opened them and fanned through the bills. They were a mix of twenties and tens and fives and a few ones. Each bag couldn't contain more than $1500 or so, he thought. There were 30 bags, so the case had $45,000 in it.

Towards the bottom he found plastic baggies of pot which was dried and brittle. He opened one and smelled it. It smelled vaguely like a skunk, but mostly it didn't have any smell left. He poured it out and it blew away in the light breeze.

At the bottom was an Adidas shoe box. He opened it and saw a variety of gold jewelry. There were rings and ear rings and pendants and chains. They were tarnished but he rubbed a heavy man's ring with this thumb and saw the gold beneath. At the bottom of the shoe box he saw a manila envelope had been folded over to fit into the box. He pulled it out and wondered what sort of documents his dad or Willie would have thought important enough to save. He gently tore through the top flap and opened the envelope. Inside, he could see photos.

The photos were of his dad, of course, and Willie, and his mother. One was a wedding photo. There were other photos of old people he didn't know. One was his dad graduating from high school. A few others were fused together. He dropped the photos back in the envelope and noticed the envelope held some sort of certificate. He carefully coaxed the certificate out of the envelope and turned it over. It was his birth certificate. There was his name: Russell Thomas Moye. He had taken his mother's name, Grimes, when he turned 18, but this was the name he was born to.

When he pulled the big truck into his garage, it was dark. He brushed his teeth and went to bed. In the morning, he took a shower. He used some expensive soap and shampoo he had bought a few weeks back. He let the hot water beat down on him for a long time and thought of the trip. It seemed like it had happened long ago.

He took the truck back to the lot and saw that Ted was already there. Ted was wiping down the Lexus.

"You're back already?" Ted asked.

"Yeah. No luck with the Lexus?" he said.

"Oh, no, it's sold," Ted said proudly. "Got the deposit late last night. She's coming back for it this afternoon."

"How much?"

"Twenty eight thousand. She didn't even try to negotiate. We had to take back her Camero, but she said she was ready to upgrade," Ted said.

"What was her name?" he asked. It couldn't be, he thought.

"Tina something," Ted said. "She asked about you. Then she saw the car and said she wanted to drive it. Then she said she wanted it."

"Good job, Ted," he said. Ted was the new manager, he decided.

He went to his office and got her phone number off the contract. She answered on the second ring.

"Are you calling about my new car?" she said. He could feel her smiling through the phone line.

"You should have waited until I was here," he said. "I could have given you a better deal".

"I'm buying a Lexus, baby! I don't want a good deal! That's my new dream car!" she squealed.

He drove it over to her that afternoon. She ran around the car clapping her hands.

He went in to see Willie. Willie didn't look well but when he leaned down and told Willie what he had done, Willie smiled. He told Willie about meeting Popper. Willie's blue eyes crackled with pride.

"Good for you, boy," he said. "Good for you."

That afternoon, he drove her Camero back to the lot and she followed in the Lexus. After she had completed her paperwork, he asked her to dinner and she said yes. That weekend, he took her out for an expensive meal and sat at a table instead of the bar. Her eyes were alive with life. He knew he was in love, and it was likely to last.

Willie died a few weeks later in his sleep. Tina called Russell, as she called him, early in the morning to tell him, and he arrived a few minutes later. She had the ambulance wait until he arrived and he rode with Willie's corpse to the hospital.

A week later, she attended Willie's funeral and held his hand. He was taking her back to work when he invited her to go to California with him. He needed to go check on a car and he wanted to tour wine country.

When she said yes, he knew one day he would marry her, and one perfect day, he did.

SCENES FROM A FRENCH POST OFFICE

Lisa told him there was a funk hanging over Germany, but he didn't pay attention to many things she said, and so the declaration was glossed over in the excitement of just going there. At the airport, he wasn't thinking about hanging funks because he was wild-eyed with wonder at regular people walking around. These were Germans, in Germany!

Shortly after getting off the train, he walked into a bar and ordered a schnitzel, and drank three beers. Later, when the idea of being out of the USA had worn off, and when Lisa was still asleep, he would get up early and walk around whatever town they were in. Slowly, he began to be able to feel it. There was something dark hanging over the place. Often, as the sun rose, he'd find himself in a cemetery behind a cathedral where there was row upon row of small headstones. They inevitably had male names etched in stone and dates such as March 1, 1915 – April 3, 1944.

But Nick had quit his job to make the trip, and he was still having a great time. Lisa and her show friends were hard drinkers and partiers, and he liked them, but his total curiosity was engaged with the places he visited. The people were all interesting mysteries. He engaged the waiters at the little hotels where they stayed. "Bitte Schon," they would say, practically clicking their heels together. That made him smile.

Her friends didn't seem to know or appreciate much about anything other than each other, and they argued a lot. The lead player in the show was black and very gay, and he would get drunk and break things. The German hotel staff started to follow him around and that made him crazy mad. Lisa was older than most of the players in the show but she mixed it up with them, smoke for smoke, drink for drink. These were her people and he didn't fit in. But, he also didn't care.

As far as the show was concerned, his timing was comically perfect. Just before he arrived, she fell off a flat during a performance, and though she limped her way through her scenes, the swelling indicated a serious problem, which was confirmed by an efficient German doctor a few days later. She had a broken the fifth metatarsal on her right foot and only surgery could bring the separated bone pieces back together.

So, she had to leave the show just weeks after Nick arrived. Simon, the British show director, was pleased that no one from the show would have to be dedicated to taking her to the city where she would get the surgery. Lisa wasn't coming back and getting her surgically repaired and gone was something he was obliged to do, but he wanted it done with the least impact on the show possible. Her muscular American boyfriend was the perfect solution to that problem.

"You're such a beautiful, beautiful man," Simon said one evening as he rubbed Nick's forearm. They were in the bar at the hotel and Lisa was not there. "And that fucking cunt Lisa gets to have you."

Nick laughed. He knew the Brits, especially the gay ones, were maudlin drunks. He made a mental note to keep his mouth shut the next time he was drunk. Booze brought out the darkness in him as well. And, gays hitting on him was nothing new.

In the last days before he had to take care of Lisa on his own, he traveled through Southern Germany. He grew to like the darkness hanging over the country. He loved the gothic lettering on the sides of buildings that functioned as street signs. He loved the food everywhere he went. He drank a lot of beer. The Germans kept to themselves. Days went by and he spoke to no one.

Finally, he went to Munich and took the streetcar to Dachau. He walked the few well-marked blocks to the former concentration camp which had served as the administrative center of the entire camp system during the Holocaust. It was, to his surprise, perfectly preserved. He wandered around reading all the placards. He made his way to the famous gate that had "Albeit Macht Frei" rendered in steel.

It's too bad, Nick thought, that the Nazis had discredited so many good ideas. In a just world, work does make you free.

He went to the Hofbrauhaus for dinner, drank three big steins of beer, and then walked back to the train station to travel back to Lisa. The rest of the trip, he knew, would be all about her.

She checked into an old hospital building made of grey stones that had high windows and were staffed by nuns in full habits. The doctor was very handsome, and she shamelessly flirted with him even when he pressed on her broken bones. Nick found a cheap hotel nearby that was cold and damp. He tried to wash his underwear and socks in the tiny sink, but in the morning they were still wet, but now cold, and still dirty.

He arrived at the hospital the morning of her surgery and she had already been returned to her room. The first thing she hissed at him when he arrived was, "You have to get me out of here!"

"Why?" he asked.

"They don't have any pain meds! They gave me aspirin," she said. He could see tears forming in her eyes. "Look at this."

She unwrapped her foot and he saw the incision; it was huge. It ran from just under the ball of the ankle forward to her pinky toe.

"Jesus…" he said. "I didn't think they'd have to make a cut that big."

"Yeah, neither did I, and it hurts like hell but these bitches won't give me anything for it," she said.

He walked out of her room and approached a desk in the hallway. At the desk, an elderly nun was reading, but she looked up when he tapped the desk. He pointed back to Lisa's room and then at his foot and spoke slowly.

"She needs something for the pain," he said.

The nun called over two other nuns, and one told him in halting English that Lisa had already been given pills for pain.

"It still hurts," he said.

"We give her another pills in two hours," the nun said with a curt smile, and then she turned and walked away.

"We're getting the fuck out of here," Lisa said when he reported what the nuns had told him. "Go to the lobby. There's a vending machine there that sells beer. Get me two of them. Then, go get your stuff, bring it back here, and we'll go."

"Go? You just got out of surgery," he said. He had seen Lisa angry before and she was not one to silently cry about anything, but this seemed like a really bad idea. "You can't walk on that foot. It will start hurting a hell of a lot more."

"That's what the beer is for. Get me three of them," she said and lay down.

"Where are we going?" he asked.

"France," she said. "They sell real drugs in the pharmacies."

Nick went to the lobby and, just as she had told him, there was the vending machine that sold beer in tall cans. He purchased three and went back to her room. She downed one before he was gone to get his stuff.

When he returned, she was dressed and had lined the empty beer cans on the window sill. Stacked in the corner were all six of her bags. Three were suitcases and three were big bags with handles. He had carried them in but the British director had helped. Now, he was on his own.

"When I get these bags out to the street," he said, "you call the cab. Do you know where we're going?"

"Yes," she said as she experimented with various ways to wrap her foot. "We're going to the coast. I want to be somewhere cool."

"The coast? That's a long way from here," he said. "How many trains is that?"

"I don't know, Nick! But I'm going and you can come if you want to!" she snapped.

This, he knew, was bullshit. If he didn't help her, she wasn't going anywhere. It was his call. He could say no and just get her enough beer until she passed out. But, he didn't want to. He wanted to see the French coast, and he also had decided that he wanted to show those German nuns what Americans will do.

This, he decided, was going to be fun.

He approached the nun at the desk. She was still reading her book.

"Hey," he said, smiling. "I need to get a rolling bed. Do you have one I could use?"

She looked over at the nun that spoke English. Nick smiled at her as well and noted that she was actually very pretty. Her strong, clean features were framed by her white coif.

"I need a rolling bed so I can roll all her bags out to the front," he said. "We're leaving."

Her smile faded and she looked confused.

"It is not possible," the nun said. "It… It is not possible."

Nick smiled. He felt good about being an American.

"It's very possible," he said and turned away.

He passed Lisa's room and went to the next room. In it was a hospital bed on wheels, so he rolled it into the hallway. He saw the nun was talking to Lisa. Two others stood in the hall watching.

"This is not possible," the nun said. "You had surgery on your fuss and cannot walk with."

"I could walk if you'd give me a decent pair of crutches," she said, waving her red crutches at the nun. They were the kind with cuffs around the forearm and not the kind with pads that went under the armpit.

While they argued back and forth, Nick started stacking her bags on the bed in the hallway. The other nuns said something in German but they made no effort to stop him. When he was done, he nodded at Lisa and she stood, adjusted her crutches, and took a painful step forward.

"OK!" the nun said. "We not stop you, but you must sign the paper, a… So that…"

The nun could not find the English words.

"A release," Lisa said. "Fine, but you better hurry up because I'm calling a taxi in the lobby, and then we're gone."

Lisa limped to the elevator and Nick rolled the bed full of bags behind her. In the lobby, she called a taxi from the payphone. They were waiting outside in the cold air when the nun arrived with a piece of paper. She handed Lisa the paper perched on a book and Lisa signed it, and the nun turned and left without a word.

And so began a long evening of relaying bags back and forth from place to place. The taxi dropped them at the train station and Nick was able to move the bags in two relays. First were the two biggest suitcases, and then he could hang the other bags around his neck and carry the remaining four in one trip. Lisa sipped on another beer and read the train map.

"We have to go from here to Cologne," she said. "From there, we go in Belgium, through Brussels, and then to Lille." She pointed to a small town in the north of France. "It's not on this map, but there'll be a train to here, to Calais."

Nick stepped up to look closer. Calais was right on the coast and was the departure point for England.

"It's right across the English Channel from the white cliffs of Dover," he said with a grin. God damn, this was fun!

On the train to Cologne, they watched the sunset. Nick could get no ice in the bar car, but he could buy more cans of cold beer. Lisa kept her foot propped on the window sill as he strapped the beer cans to her foot with a scarf. When the chill had worn off the beer, they would drink them.

The Cologne train station was open and cool, and from the platform, Nick could see the lights of the giant two-towered Cologne cathedral. When she and her bags were positioned on the correct platform, and he had waited outside the bathroom for her and she had sat back down and started to doze off, he walked out of the station and across the Platz to the cathedral.

It was lit up and magnificent. In so many ways, it was the opposite of the Christianity he had absorbed as a child in the Baptist South. The cathedral was an object of beauty, worthy all by itself. It was meant to dwarf people and it succeeded. He stood in front of it and just stared, trying to drink in as much of the experience as he could while he could. Soon, he'd be back to taking care of Lisa.

They boarded the next train after a long wait. Lisa had a hang-over and was sleepy and in pain and couldn't drink any more beer.

He positioned her by the window and, after securing all of her bags, propped her legs in his lap and went to sleep. The train was a beehive of activity, however, as it stopped in many towns and many people got on and off. There were multiple languages spoken in the hall outside of their cabin and the smell of Middle Eastern food and sweat. He would open his eyes when new people sat down beside them.

When they reached Brussels, he had to wake her. The Brussels train station was full of people, even in the middle of the night, and she was now in a lot of pain. Moving her bags became even more difficult because he couldn't leave the first two sitting too far away while he moved the rest. So, he'd move two the length of a hallway, get the other four, then move the next distance, and so on, until they reached the ticket office. Lisa had to dig through three bags until she found both her passport and money. Everything Nick had brought was in a single backpack.

The train from Brussels to France was even more crowded and the Middle Easterners crowded onto the train and closed the doors to their compartment even if the seats were not full. Lisa stood in the narrow hallway as Nick opened each compartment door, looking for a one with two empty seats. The Middle Easterners waved their arms and yelled and one man stood up to close the door, but Nick stopped him with a palm to his chest plus a sharp and threatening, "Back off!"

"I'm going to deck one of these motherfucking rag heads," Nick said loud enough for everyone else to hear.

He found a seat for her and set the smaller of her bags in a pile and then went to stow the rest. When he came back, he found Lisa arguing with a man over her bags in the seat. Nick settled it by pushing the bags to the floor and sitting down. The man grumbled and moved on.

Once the train was moving, Nick went to the bar car for more beer. It was warm and not useful to her foot, but she drank it anyway and drifted back to sleep.

At sunrise, the train arrived at the Lille station and he woke Lisa. She was surly and uncooperative, but he got her to the platform, stacked the bags around her, and went looking for something to eat. The station had a busy McDonald's, but he had no francs, only marks, so he had to wait an hour until the teller windows opened at a nearby bank to get the money needed to buy the food.

After she ate, Lisa finally cracked a smile. "I'm so happy not to be back in that hospital," she said. "Fuck those nuns and Germany."

They laughed. "It is not possible!" they both said over and over and giggled.

She directed him to go outside the station and see if he saw the neon plus sign that indicated a French pharmacy and he saw one less than a block away. When he told her, she smiled again. He waited with the bags while she limped off to the pharmacy. A half-hour later, she returned with several sheets of pop-out pills. She gave him one when he reported that his back hurt from moving all the bags around. She took four. They dozed while they waited for the noon train to Calais.

They caught a taxi at the Calais train station and she directed the driver to take them to the cheapest hotel on the beach. The driver dropped them off at a low rectangular building that looked like the top of a cruise ship sticking out of the sand. The hotel was mostly empty and the French staff was lethargic and sullen. No one offered to help him with the bags, but after a short time, they were in a hotel room. When she lay down on the bed, he started to undress her. She was in a good mood. He climbed on top of her, being careful not to kick around too much because that made her foot hurt.

That afternoon, while she slept, he walked down to the beach and discovered that the coast was dotted with the ruins of the Nazi coastal defenses. These had not been destroyed during the war since it had been the Normandy beaches that took the beating. The Calais defenses had been abandoned and later, tides and wind caused many of them to collapse. Now, they were empty and unguarded.

He climbed in and out of the pillboxes and scrambled over the sea walls as he made his way down the beach. He was very happy. He thought again about how he was always able to find special places, and do things that meant something special to him, but always when he was alone. Lisa wouldn't have been with him even if she could walk. His friend Bill was the only one who shared his knack for special places.

That evening they went to dinner in town and the lights sparkled in the cafes and along the boulevards. The drugs had worked and Lisa was in a fine mood. They decided on Mediterranean food and had goat, lamb, and hummus plus lots of fine Belgian beer.

Lisa ordered in French with confidence. She chattered on and laughed a lot and he remembered why he liked her. But after a few beers, he remembered that he didn't love her, that he had never longed for her. She had always been a target of opportunity for him, and she had only recently offered him a chance to go to Europe for the first time, and now he was taking care of her. Or at least, he was taking care of her luggage.

That night, back at the hotel, they had sex again. She carefully climbed on top which was how she liked it. Nick knew just where and how to touch her to make her moan and lean her head back. Afterward, she fell over and went to sleep, and he got up and went down to the dark beach again. It was a three-quarter moon and clear, and finally, he could the lights across the channel. He hoped in the morning, it would be clear enough to see the white chalky cliffs of Dover.

But, instead, a fog settled in and things were not clear at all in the morning. Lisa was hung over, and since she was in a foul mood, he figured it was as good a time as any to address his plan for her bags.

He suggested that they box up at least some of her stuff and mail it back to her parent's house in Florida. They had tickets out of Amsterdam, but they couldn't leave for another two weeks and he didn't want to stay in one place or relay her bags every time they moved. Most of the bags contained clothes, and they could be shipped, he suggested.

After some swearing, she tentatively agreed, and so he walked to town and looked in the alleys behind the restaurants until he had collected the right-sized boxes. He tucked them under his arm and took them back to the hotel.

She spent the rest of the morning separating clothes and packing the boxes. He went back to the beach. The tide was low and the fog was thick. A few British families were out, and they walked through the mist collecting shells. The men had their pants legs rolled up and kids splashed around in their shorts. He heard fog horns from the boats in the channel.

In the afternoon, he returned to their room and saw that she had reduced her load to just the two suitcases. The rest of the bags were consolidated to just the two boxes. He took a shower and when she woke, she showered as well while he went downstairs to talk to the fussy concierge about where to find the nearest post office. When he went back to their room, she was standing naked in the bathroom drying her hair, and that led quickly to the bed where they had sex again for a long time. She smelled clean and delicious.

Nick carried the boxes downstairs and they took a taxi to the post office. Lisa went inside while he took the boxes out of the trunk of the taxi. The Middle Eastern taxi driver didn't help or get out of his seat and Nick threw the fare at him through the open window. The driver muttered something in another language and drove away.

"Asshole," Nick whispered.

He carried the boxes inside and set them down beside Lisa, but then noticed she was speaking broken French with a frantic tone.

"What's wrong?" he asked. She ignored him. The postal lady was shaking her head. Lisa took a step back.

"Well, fuck you!" Lisa yelled at the woman and then she turned and hobbled towards the door.

"What's happening? " Nick asked.

Other French postal workers emerged from the back offices, and they were watching Nick warily. Lisa struggled to push the heavy front door open.

"They want $170 for each box," she said. A tear rolled down her cheek.

"What? Really? Why?" he asked.

She stopped pushing on the door and poked him in the leg with one of her crutches.

"Because things are expensive here, Nick! That's the way it is and you should have known that!" she yelled.

"How was I supposed to know?" he yelled back.

More postal workers gathered. A small crowd was collecting for the show.

"All I wanted to do was make it easier for us to travel around," he continued

"You didn't think I wanted to it be easier?" she said. "I broke my foot! So, I'm sorry! And all you've done is complain about the bags ever since."

Now Nick was mad. He had not wanted to relay her luggage across Europe, but he had done so and not ever declined any wish she expressed, from leaving the hospital early to fetching beer from the bar cars. To claim otherwise was a deep insult.

"That's bullshit!" he protested. "I moved all of it through hospitals and train stations in three countries and I never said a word!"

"Yes, you did!" she said.

"No, Lisa, I did not," he said. "You're thinking of the other guy who's been taking care of you since you had surgery."

She surveyed the scene and let out a final "Fuck you all!" and then swung at Nick's head with the crutch. He swatted it away hard enough to knock it out of her hand. She pushed the door open and hobbled out on one crutch.

For a moment, he watched her list down the sidewalk as fast as she could go. She wobbled back and forth, leaning heavily on the one crutch she still had. He almost laughed but didn't. He picked up her other crutch and left.

He followed along behind her for a block. She glanced over her shoulder after a few minutes and saw him but didn't stop. After another painful block, she reached a park bench and sat down. She winced and lifted her broken foot to the bench.

He caught up and sat down beside her and then handed her the other crutch.

"Fuck you," she said calmly.

"I'll go get your stuff," he said. "It'll be OK. We'll find a way to get it home."

"No way," she said. "I'd rather lose it all than see that look on your face every time you have to touch it."

He started to protest, then thought better of it. He hadn't complained, but she had seen his agitation with her bags and it was the same thing as complaining about them.

Nick looked behind them and saw there was a tiny pub with a Union Jack sticker on the door. This meant they spoke English inside. She hobbled inside and they had several beers and then ordered a plate of hummus and pita. By sundown, they were back in their room, and she quickly fell asleep.

They spent several days in Amsterdam. Nick wandered the streets by himself and stopped at the Anne Frank house. He arrived shortly before they were closing for the day and was alone in the tiny bedroom where Anne Frank composed one of the great odes to youth and romance. In this tiny space, she had lived and found romance with the only boy available. Nick knew that he had the whole world and throngs of romantic choices, and he still could not find joy.

He stood in front of the Hollywood movie stars she had pasted to her wall and thought about the immense influence his country's culture had on the rest of the world.

They locked the door behind him when he left. He looked down the Prinsengracht canal at the fading light and heard the bells at the Westerkerk behind him. What happened to whoever ratting Anne Frank out, he wondered. Was there a funk hanging over that family? Where wasn't there a funk? Everywhere he'd ever been had a funk hanging over it, and if you stayed in one place long enough, you'd feel it.

When they returned to the states, he rented a car and drove her down to Sarasota, and delivered her to her parent's house. Her mom and dad had kept her room the same since she was in high school, though that had been the better part of two decades. They had quiet sex a final time the night before he left.

When he returned to California, the scene in the French post office made a good story. People laughed. Bill knew Lisa as well and he rolled his eyes and didn't ask any questions. After a while, Nick's attention drifted back to the movie business and the lifestyle he and Bill had created and he didn't think about Lisa at all.

A HIKE

Lydia had driven across town from Silver Lake to meet Nick at his apartment in Santa Monica. It was a Saturday so there was no traffic. Constantly taking her out to dinner was getting to be expensive, so he asked her to come to his place, and then they would go hiking. He had suggested Will Rodgers State Park and she didn't object. She had never been there and he had been going there since his days in art school. It was an easy hike and involved no pre-planning, and it didn't take very long.

If he went to Silver Lake, he knew they would have sex. He had only been to her place a few times and they had sex on her sofa each time. She lived in a small apartment in an Art Deco-era building that was clean and well kept. She lived by herself and had no roommates and no pets to take into consideration. They would eat, talk, and then the clothes would come off.

After sex, she would gather her clothes off the floor and head off to the bathroom and he could get an unobstructed view of her standing body, which was very nice. She was young, but she didn't work out, so there was none of the muscle tone that comes with running or Pilates or whatever the ladies were doing. There were just the familiar curves of the female form in its most native state. He liked that. He was obsessive about exercise but didn't want a woman who was the same.

It was summer now, and she was coming to Santa Monica where it was hazy and cool. A mist hung in the air, diffusing the light and making everything bright and harsh to the eye.

As he drank his coffee in the dirty kitchen, he heard a thump above him. Bill had just gotten up. Then there was the toilet flush and then the heavy bounding down the stairs.

"Going out with that slut?" Bill asked.

"Hiking at Will Rodgers," said Nick.

"Hope a bear doesn't bite your face off," Bill replied.

Bill made himself a cup of coffee.

"But you know what they say; you don't have to run faster than the bear, just faster than your date," he said.

A pervading sarcasm was Bill's comic method.

Bill started to clean the kitchen and put away the dishes in the sink and rinse the pots and pans he had used the previous night to make a big meal. They had invited a few people over and it had turned into a party. The house had been full of friends. Nick had laughed and laughed. Everyone had crammed into the kitchen and danced.

Now the place was trashed. Nick picked up a few things on the counter, put them in the overflowing trash, and took the trash out to the dumpster in the alley.

As he was walking back in, he saw Lydia arrive. He watched her through the bougainvillea as she gathered her things and applied a bit of lip gloss. She was a fine-looking woman. As he watched her, he thought about the party last night. There were some smart ladies there, but Lydia was young, sexually available, and low maintenance. It was what he wanted, and he was hooked.

When she entered the townhouse, Bill was just finishing up in the kitchen. He leaned against the counter, still in his boxers, and took a long, loud sip of coffee, but he didn't offer her any.

They exchanged an icy greeting and Nick said goodbye to Bill and hustled her to the door. Bill was always rude to his dates, so Nick didn't think anything of it.

He opened the door to his truck for her and as she passed, he could smell her. She smelled of bath lotions and hair care products. These smells always sent a jolt to his heart and he wanted to lean in and nuzzle her neck, but he didn't.

He drove down to Ocean Drive and then down the big ramp to the PCH and headed north. They would go to the bottom of Sunset Blvd and then make their way up to the entrance to the park.

The windows were down and he could feel the moist ocean air.

"It's cold," she said after a moment, so he rolled his window up and turned on the heat. That appeared to satisfy her, but it was hard to tell; she was never much of a talker and while she had dark auburn hair and thick eyebrows, and a hint of olive skin, she was cool in temperament and not one to go into detail about anything. She had a Mediterranean look and a Scandinavian outlook. She was perfect.

In the enclosed cab of the truck, he was able to detect the one thing about her that repelled him; she had horrible breath. It couldn't be tasted, but it could be smelled. He had no plans to ever say anything to her about it.

As they reached the bottom of Sunset, he looked out over the ocean. The Pacific always seemed so calm, even when the surf was up. The

Gulf of Mexico where he grew up was a hateful witch, always changing personalities and ready at an instant to well up and destroy. Whitecaps in the distance were normal on the Gulf of Mexico, but he never saw anything on the horizon of the Pacific. It either had nothing to offer or didn't care. They were more likely to be hit by a mudslide or a wildfire coming from the east than anything coming from the west.

"You know what they say about the Pacific?" he asked her, sure she would have no opinion even though she was from San Diego and had spent her whole life on this very ocean.

"What?"

"It has no memory," he offered. The look on her face gave away nothing.

They turned right on Sunset and made their way past a giant windmill. The blades of a windmill reached up from the dense gardens surrounding it. Nick turned to look back at the lake at the base of the windmill.

"That was a movie set, from way back in the twenties, and now it's some kind of new-age church," he said.

She turned her head to look. He had heard that it was once the home of Fatty Arbuckle, and he started to tell her about it, but then declined; he didn't want to explain who Fatty Arbuckle was. For a fleeting moment he thought how uninterested in the history of her region she was, or her chosen industry for that matter. He met her at the movie studio and quickly discovered that, unlike his friends, she knew nothing and cared little about movies. Her job there was just a job.

He knew all about his native culture, the type of people who lived there, where they came from, and the wars and losses and reeking land that never forgot a thing. The whole culture at home smelled like her breath. He wished he knew less.

She was lovely to look at, he thought, and that was enough. That she was as cold as the ocean she grew up around seemed to suit him somehow. He expected little, and he got it.

When they reached Will Rodgers State Park, they saw polo ponies on the field and kids, mostly girls, riding horses back and forth. The girls held their mallets high and tried to lean down to hit the ball, but they were just too short and the horses too tall.

Nick chuckled at the kids leaning far over the side of the horses as their mothers or caretakers rushed out to provide directions and encouragement.

"They need smaller horses or they need to play the game with beach balls," he said.

On the way up the hill, they passed the big ranch house where Will Rodgers once lived. The main doors were open, and inside, there were cowboy memorabilia on display as well as a life-sized carving of the famed humorist. The wooden Will Rodgers was smiling and looking down. He looked happy and wise. He had lived well.

Nick stopped and leaned in the door. The house was big, cool, empty, and quiet. He turned and looked at Lydia, but she was still looking toward the ponies, and he saw her glance at her watch.

They made their way towards the stables in the back, and then up the winding road towards the top of the hill. He had been here many times and knew which trailhead to take. Some trails went straight up to the top but they were narrow and hard to traverse, and she was not wearing boots.

So, they took the easy but long way. After a few minutes, he could see a line of sweat forming on her upper lip. It was sexy. He dropped back a little and interlaced his fingers with hers. She looked out towards the ocean.

As they neared the top, they came to the trailhead for the path that worked its way north. This was the Backbone Trail and it worked its way through the Santa Monica Mountains all the way to Santa Barbara. He and Bill had hiked it in as far as they dared and it had been a great day of fun. He decided not to suggest he and Lydia try it.

Finally, they reached the summit which normally provided a vista from Catalina to Pasadena. But, it was still hazy and wincing white with the sun bouncing every which way through the water vapor in the air. They could see back to the ponies below, but not out to the ocean and barely to Santa Monica, and certainly not to Silver Lake or Catalina.

"We're a little early," he said. "The sun will burn off this haze eventually."

There was a family there, but after a few minutes, the father announced it was time to leave and the kids ran down the path. After that, Nick and Lydia were alone.

They sat on the only bench and stared into the blinding haze. He put his arm around her and tried to peer through the white gauze of light to see if he could spot any of downtown, but he couldn't.

Suddenly, she stood, faced him, and backed away a couple of steps. She took in a deep breath and in the brief instant that followed, he determined that whatever she was about to say or do, it was something planned. He was about to hear something that had been rehearsed.

"Look," she started, "I've been thinking about this and I've decided that I don't love you and I never could. You're a good person, but we don't need to keep doing this."

Nick just stared at her for a long moment. His arm was along the back of the bench, in the same position it had been when it was around her shoulders seconds ago. Now he was staring at her darkened face which was outlined by the haze. He could barely make out her features but could tell she was looking at the ground.

"You waited until we got all the way up here to tell me that?" he asked. "Why didn't you say something before?"

"I don't know," she said. "I was waiting for the right time."

"Well, this is not it," he said. "It's going to be a long hike down, that's for sure."

He was right; it was a long tense hike back down. He walked quickly and stayed a few paces ahead of her. He'd stop now and again and wait for her to catch up, and then start walking in long, determined strides again.

The ride back went fast. He didn't go back down to the ocean. Instead, he went further up Sunset to Bundy and then through the residential section of the Palisades back to Santa Monica.

The goodbye was perfunctory. A bit of the sting had died down for the moment and he wanted to maintain a decent bearing so he gave her a light hug and went inside. He heard her car door shut as he was opening his door.

Bill was on the couch eating cereal, still in his boxers.

"That was fast," he said.

Nick went to the kitchen and found an open bottle of cheap wine from the night before. He poured himself a big glass, then pushed Bill's legs aside, and plopped down on the huge sofa next to him.

"We broke up," he said. "She waited until we got all the way up to the overlook to tell me. It was miserable. Worst hike ever."

Bill snorted and then laughed.

"She's a slut," Bill chortled. "Good riddance. Now we can start having fun again! Yeah! Nicky's back!"

Bill kicked Nick with one of his giant feet causing Nick to spill his wine.

"Watch out, bastard!" he said. But he was laughing again. Bill never wandered off with a woman of his own.

Later, they went out for groceries and then went to the gym. But as he waited for Bill to finish a set, he thought about the hilltop at Will

Rodgers State Park. The sting was still there, and he hoped she hadn't ruined that location for him. He had been there many times, and the place held a rare sunny spot in his memory, and now a new memory had taken hold. He didn't want to remember it, but he knew he would.

SAFETY SWITCH

She had moved her things to California by getting rid of a lot of stuff and packing the rest into a U-Hail trailer. After the wedding, they went to her mother's house, but after a time, Nick left since the mood was so tense and she packed up everything with the help of her cousin. The next day, they drove her car west on I-10 pulling the trailer. Bill, who had been his best man, left for home and they were alone for at next three days.

Nick had covered this road many times before. He did a quick memory check and determined that this was his twelfth crossing of North America in a car. He had crossed on I-40, had traveled the I-70, had spent time on I-15, but most of the trip had been on I-10. Now he was married, she was his wife, and they were pulling all of her possessions in a trailer.

It was 114 degrees when they drove through Arizona but the time passed quickly and soon they were crawling west through the cities that lead to Los Angeles. They passed through the shadow of the Bonaventure Hotel and then reached the end of I-10 in Santa Monica.

It was a week from Christmas when they had come across each other by happenstance. She caught him up on all the people he had not seen since high school. At the end of the night, they snuck into the football stadium. In high school, she had outranked him, but now their social 'X' had crossed. They began to kiss, and then right in the front row, in the empty stadium on a December evening, they had sex on the concrete bleachers.

So, he had fallen hard. And now nine months had passed and they were in Santa Monica in the townhome he shared with Bill. And now, she was going crazy. She was raging.

She learned to hate Bill. Bill was amused, but, as was his style, he didn't say much. As the romantic hazy quickly burned away, Nick was shocked at what he had done and he told Bill he was sorry for bringing it all to an end. She burst into rages the likes he had never seen and her rage was now the dominant factor in Nick's life. A brief window of friendship and happiness, a period away from women and their troubles, had opened, and Nick had slammed it shut for a girl from high school. He was shocked at what he had done. Bill was just sad, and when he was drunk, even sadder, but that was it.

After a few miserable weeks in Santa Monica, Nick and his wife moved to their own apartment. Nick hoped this would calm her down and she would be who she had presented herself to be. The apartment was on the ground floor and was small, but it was in Culver City, near the movie studio where he worked. But, she was still hopping mad most of the time, and her religious roots began to show more clearly. She started to read and quote the Bible more frequently. She would go silent when he would slip his shoes on to go for a run in the evenings; she didn't want him going out.

But, there was something more grown-up about being married and he had been reaching for grownup status for a long time. Now, he had it. He had adulthood, every day, good and hard. Grownups take trips together, so he took her to a ranch in Santa Barbara, which was another place grownups of means went.

They stayed in a cabin with simple furnishings. The whole idea was not to be inside so they wouldn't argue. They walked around on the grounds and Nick stared longingly at the mountains in the distance. They looked like picture-postcard mountains, but they were real, he had hiked many of them with Bill, they were always beautiful, and he always wanted to be near them.

There was always sex to bring them together, so Nick had sex with his wife before they went to dinner. She got angry before they left so she went out of the cabin to smoke. They ate, walked some more, he took some pictures, and then they settled in for a night of restless sleep.

Christmas passed and they were alone. On Christmas morning, they opened some gifts, and then Nick started thinking about going out and getting some air. Bill was back East and she was happier when he was not around. Christmas marked a year since they had been reacquainted, and he noted that bitterly as she grew angry again. Whatever sexual burn had been present had cooled. Now there was the heat of her anger and the chemical burn of his resentment at her anger, and little else.

By February, she was pregnant. The trip to Santa Barbara was back-dated and identified as the place. This came as a shock to Nick. She had told him she could not have kids when they met, and he had accepted that. Now, she was pregnant.

Trips to the doctor were scheduled at regular intervals. It was a strange and alien landscape for Nick, who never got sick, had no friends with kids, and didn't miss any of it.

But now, he was waiting in the OB's office and then going back with her and watching the nurse smear a clear gel on his wife's belly and then apply the big ultrasound wand.

In the grainy black and white field on the screen which represented her uterus, there was an egg in a pan. It was unmistakable as was the motion in the yolk of the egg that was accompanied by the swishing sound pumped out of speakers over their heads. He was looking at and hearing a beating heart. Not his own, or hers, but that of a tiny creature set in motion inside her.

The fighting subsided. She was still miserable about most things, but her mind was occupied with what her new circumstances meant. She told him things about herself that he never knew, and they were very unflattering things about what she had done in the nearly two decades between when he had known her in high school and when they had met a year ago. She was thinking about her predicament and her life and so she had less energy to attack him.

Bill took the news quietly. He was drinking more and he kept the same music playing in the old townhome. They went out for beers and talked about other things. There were few congratulations. It was not like when they announced they were getting married. Everyone who had seen what the past few months had brought did not anticipate that a baby would make any of it better.

But Nick warmed to the idea of a baby. He was amazed at the progress of the blur on the ultrasound screen. He quickly grew used to her complaining about whatever was oozing out of her and they both enjoyed talking about names.

Trips to the doctor became routine, and he learned where to park, how long it would take to walk to the doctor's office, and she learned the names of all the women who worked there.

Finally, they had something in common. This project didn't involve Bill, their home, his work, or anything else. It was something they were creating together and it was happening without further input from either of them so there was no arguing. If they had to design a baby together, they would have mud wrestled over the details, but this child was charging forward without input from either of them. They still fought, she still got plenty mad, Bill still wasn't very excited, and life was not utterly changed, except in Nick. He had become a dad, at least on the inside.

She called him at work in a panic, which wasn't unusual. She was bleeding, and wanted to go to the OB office immediately.

"How much are you bleeding?" he asked and that agitated her greatly. She had called the OB office, and now she wanted him to come get her.

The doctor was an Asian woman, but it was mostly white women who worked there. Mostly Hispanic women were waiting in the lobby. She didn't see the doctor on most visits, she just saw the nurses who did the ultra sound. They had told her she could come in any time she wanted, and she wanted to go often. She worried and the ultra sound calmed her, so Nick would take her whenever she asked.

He dropped her off at the front door and parked. On the way over, she had worried and wrung her hands, and he had rolled his eyes, which she saw. She was freaking out, and he had seen this reaction many times before, so he was not overly worried.

She waited for him to arrive before going to the ultrasound room. They were escorted back and she chatted busily with the nurse. Nick marveled at the way she could turn it on for the nurses. She could turn on the smiles and giggles at will, he had learned, and he knew he had been played like a fiddle when they met. He lived with the real her, and most everyone else got the version the nurses knew. That's the way he saw it. Bill had seen the real her as had a couple others. Anyone who saw that person did not forget.

She put the hospital gown on and then removed her pants and lay down. This was not the room they were usually in, and it had few places for Nick to sit. He moved over to the far side of the room and sat on the window ledge. It was hazy in Los Angeles, and he tried to see back to his office at the movie studio but couldn't. It was whiteout conditions outside and the mist dispersed the noon sunlight. She was still talking, but he wasn't listening. After a moment, he picked up a magazine someone had left on the floor and flipped aimlessly through it. The nurse was warming up the ultrasound and smearing the gel on her stomach.

As he flipped through the pages of the magazine, he noticed the silence and looked up. His eyes came directly to the egg in the pan on the grainy ultrasound screen. It wasn't moving. The swish where the heart beat had been was still. The nurse's face told the story. It wasn't a mistake. It was over. He looked to his wife and she was paralyzed.

There were a couple of perfunctory efforts to look from another angle, but after a while, the doctor came in. She knew the story as well. It was certain. No more baby.

"About twenty five percent of pregnancies end in miscarriage," the doctor said. "It's not uncommon and it's nothing that you did."

Nick's wife was stunned to silence.

"Why?" Nick asked.

The doctor looked over to him for the first time.

"We don't know," she said. "The body has a way of deciding things. If there were abnormalities in the baby, the body shuts it down. That's our best guess. It's like a safety switch."

The 'D and C' was scheduled for the following morning. When he asked what that stood for, the nurse said "dilate and clear," without looking up from her monitor. He could do the math and knew then it was an abortion.

As they drove home, she was completely quiet. He thought of the things she had told him about herself in the weeks after she became pregnant, including the abortion she had had when she was 17. The waxen look on her face told the rest of the tale.

That night, they did not fight.

OUT OF BODY EXPERIENCE

Days dragged on and became months. The months turned to years. They added up quickly.

Nick knew that kids need order, that they thrive on routine, and doing the same thing the same way day after day delights them. Their world makes sense to them that way and they enjoy knowing what will come next.

Nick knew what would come next, and it made him ache with loneliness. As much as he loved to watch his son jump up and down on the couch, and he delighted in tickling the child, the day by day of this life was not joyful. It was barely interesting and sometimes hurt. Often, it hurt a great deal.

But, he had reverted to his earliest training now and was living out exactly what his father had done. It was as if the structure of adult life had merely been submerged for a while when he was young and full of dreams. Now, the tide had receded and revealed the rocky shores beneath.

Fear had driven him to a sales job which he excelled at. While he did not know it about himself before, he had come to find he had the gift of gab that holds the attention of others. When he spoke now, he often spoke with a certain air of authority. Travels and interesting tales gave his sentences a certain knowing ring and many people were susceptible to his stories. He even seemed a bit glamorous to some.

He was an adult success now. He had all the trappings of adulthood. He had a mortgage on a medium-sized house with three bedrooms and several oak trees that rained down leaves that needed to be raked. He had two cars, and one was a new Toyota. He had a 401K plan, and some excess cash that had been put in a CD.

And he had a child, and he had a wife.

Bill was only a few hours away, and he drove over to Bill's townhouse now and again. Bill had headed back East shortly after Nick left California. They would watch TV and crack wise and laugh about people they knew. Bill would cook and they would drink cheap wine and everything was more normal and fun. When Nick would talk about his marriage, Bill would change the subject or just say nothing. It irritated Nick at first, but later, it was one of the things that he liked about Bill. Bill, to his relief, wouldn't wallow with him.

His wife hated Bill. They had gotten along well enough at first. Bill knew about Nick and women, and this one seemed normal enough, but neither knew what was coming. As the wedding veil fell away, the person underneath it came to view. She planned to dominate Nick's time, attitudes, plans, and friends. Bill played into her hands by getting drunk and saying some drunken things about how much he was going to miss Nick.

So, for years, Nick would grow agitated when his wife would imply, and then sometimes openly state, that Bill was gay and there was something inappropriate about their relationship. Of course, there wasn't, but she said it often nonetheless. He grew to hide from her when he was going to see Bill, and then spring it on her at the last minute, which made her agitation worse. But by telling her at the last minute, he had to endure her punishment for a shorter time.

Bill didn't want to hear about any of it. He had little to say when Nick told him his wife had scratched his face.

"It comes down to the fact that I didn't get her a birthday card," he said, and Bill just snorted.

She didn't have a job and so when she spent money, she made a point of telling him how good she was with money. He said little about this and kept an accurate log of what she spent which she didn't know about. She wasn't that good.

As her birthday approached, he asked her what she wanted since she didn't deal well with surprises and he didn't want to surprise her anyway. Many birthdays and several Christmases and an equal number of Valentine's Days had taught him that these things offered more opportunities to lose than to win. They were like a roadside sobriety test; the best case was he moved on and the worst case was he went to jail and the DUI followed him around like a back injury for years and years.

"What I want," she said, speaking slowly and with long pauses, "is to be able to go to the mall and spend $200 guilt-free."

He agreed with a smile. That seemed like a painless way to pass the birthday milestone. He had told her throughout the marriage that he wanted her to be more emotionally independent and this was, from his view, her taking responsibility for her birthday happiness. All he had to do was pay.

The day of her birthday was Sunday, and he was up first with the boy. She followed about an hour later.

"Happy birthday," he said as she passed him on the way to the coffee. She wasn't a morning person, as she often pointed out, so her non-reaction wasn't abnormal.

But as they dressed for church, she projected irritation. The boy was dressed and put in the car seat, and Nick backed down the driveway.

"What is wrong with you?" he asked after a few minutes of silence and a glance at her stony profile.

The problem, he came to find out, what that he had not gotten her a birthday card. When he said he thought that his work was done when he agreed to the shopping spree, she drilled down deep with her A-list of grievances. He was selfish, he was mean, he was self-absorbed, and he should have known that cards were important to her since she got one for him on every milestone special day.

"But that's the thing," he said, his voice rising in pitch. "They don't mean anything to me. A simple 'Happy Birthday' or 'Merry Christmas' is enough. If you want to get them for me, you can do that for you, but I've told you they don't mean that much to me."

There were more invectives until they reached the church, at which point she put on another face and another voice and they went inside. In Sunday school, she touched his shoulder and called him 'sweetie' and got him some eggs from the pot luck breakfast buffet.

But by afternoon, the morning version had returned with a vengeance. It made him tired and after more bickering, which consisted of him desperately pointing out that he had done his part, and her pointing out that he refused to 'validate' her and see it from her perspective and just get her a card, he went into the bedroom to take a nap.

What he said next, he would later not remember. He had exited the kitchen with some mutterings and she had responded with some insults, and then he went into the bedroom and was taking his shoes off. Suddenly, she came through the bedroom door in an out-of-body rage and raked her clawed hand down his face.

He pushed her backward and she growled like an alley cat. His face stung and he could feel the marks crossing his eyebrow and then onto the cheek.

"What is wrong with you?" he said and touched his face. The tiny smear of blood on his finger confirmed that she had, in fact, scratched his face and she had left a mark.

As her temper cooled, she said she was sorry. She wanted to put alcohol on his face but he forbid it and told her she had done quite enough.

A couple of days later, he received a call from the pastor at the church. She had spoken to the pastor about what she had done. She wanted him to call and inform Nick about how sorry she was, so the pastor called and said she had a repentant heart.

Nick didn't laugh at the pastor, but he knew the man. The pastor was young and full of earnestness but knew little of what was in her heart.

Nick made an excuse to the people at work when asked about his face. "I cut a branch off a tree and it fell right on me!" he said and everyone rolled their eyes and laughed.

The days clocked by with the same velocity as the marks on his face slowly went away. She was less surly for a while but as he stood in the kitchen drinking coffee and watching the boy drink chocolate milk and watch *The Disney Channel*, he thought about the next storm that would brew within her and break. The fact that he didn't know what the issue would be, that it could be anything, something he currently did not know of, was defeating. He wondered why women had become so angry.

Later, he and Bill went snorkeling at the headwaters of a spring-fed river. The river poured out of the ground at a bowl-shaped opening surrounded by old hardwoods layered with dripping Spanish moss. The water was cold and as clear as the air. Bill knew about it, of course, and took Nick there. It was a long drive through the tall silent pines to the river. They changed clothes in the lavish public bathrooms that were part of a Depression-era lodge built near the springs.

"Everywhere we go," Nick said, "there's always one of these lodges built before World War Two."

"Those were good times in America," Bill said. "Back when we used to build things to last."

The river flowed from the giant hole in the ground which was very deep. They swam out to the middle and hovered over the vents that gushed fresh spring water from the bottom. Nick took a deep breath and swam down as hard and fast as he could but the bottom would get no closer. It was a long way down, and no matter how hard he tried, he wouldn't get there. Bill laughed at the way Nick's skin would ripple as he rose to the surface.

"It's so clear. It's like you're hovering over it all," he said to Bill.

"The water magnifies everything. You'll never make it all the way to the bottom," Bill said.

They sat on the grass and drank beer from a can and ate some ham sandwiches Bill had prepared. Nick's skin still tingled from the cold water. Bill was quiet. The beer was getting warm which made it bitter, but that was OK; it was still beer.

BROTHER FROM ANOTHER MOTHER

My life started when my half-brother showed up for dinner in the long summer after I graduated from high school. From my bedroom, I heard my mom greet him at the kitchen door. "Tommy! What a surprise! Come on in!" I heard her say. Even though she and my dad had been married for 14 years and Tommy had disappointed them both in a myriad of ways, she always seemed like she was trying to not be the stereotypical stepmom.

My dad married his high school sweetheart before he met my mom, so I had two older half-siblings by that union. Dara was the oldest and she was thoroughly fed up with her mother when her parents divorced. She bonded with my mom instantly and embraced her wholeheartedly. Tommy was younger and had been closer to his mother than Dara. He took the divorce hard. Consequently, he was "a lost soul" as my dad would say when he was drunk.

Tommy played football and baseball in high school and then in junior college, but he was neither big enough nor disciplined enough to compete at the college level. He drifted out of college by the end of his teens and started working outside most of the time. He did yard work, painted condominiums, and drove a delivery truck.

He would come live with us when his mother was in a rage, but then he'd drift back to her. Tommy cried a lot because his mother was so mean. When he was a little older, and he started to steal things and lie, my dad let him get away with it. My dad became a heavy drinker during this period and when he got a DUI, he had to go to mandatory counseling. The counselor pointed out that he parented Tommy out of guilt and he knew it was true.

Things changed when Tommy's mom died. She had a heart attack and just dropped dead. My dad didn't have to protect Tommy from her anymore. When I was eight, Tommy moved in with us full time, but he'd smoke in his room which drove my dad nuts. When Tommy started to drive, he hit the mailbox, a tree, and the back wall in the garage, so my dad refused to let him use any of the cars.

Tension mounted in the house and eventually, there was a huge blow-up where Tommy's rage poured out. He called my dad an asshole, my mom a home-wrecking bitch, and he threw an ashtray at me. Then there was a fistfight that my dad won. Tommy ran out the front door and we didn't see him again for a long time.

He called from jail a couple of years later. My dad got him a lawyer but didn't bail him out. Tommy did some time on a minor drug charge and was put on probation. That didn't work, so he went back to jail for three and a half years. That worked. It had been several years since Tommy had been in jail when he stopped by unannounced. My mother greeted him and invited him to stay for dinner.

He was friendly to me but I still didn't like him very much, so I avoided eye contact. He kept asking me questions about what I was doing so I told him I was looking for a job.

"If you want to make some real money, come down to the port," he said. "I can get you a job there."

"What do they do?" I asked.

"They work in the ships loading and unloading stuff," he said. "It's man's work, but I think you can handle it!" He laughed and looked over at my mom to confirm that it was funny.

"It's dangerous," she said. "That's what you said when you were going to work there."

"He'll be fine. He's all grown up now!" Tommy said. "Hey, it's 18 dollars an hour."

"You work there?" I asked.

"Hell, yeah," he said. "Not full-time, but I pick up shifts. You got to be in the union to work there full time."

"You make 18 dollars an hour?" I asked. I was skeptical; Tommy exaggerated things often.

"Yeah, I make more than that depending on what they have me doing," he said. "If you're on a gang, and they've got you working down in the hole, you make 18, but if you operate a crane or a forklift, you make more like 22."

I liked the sound of 18 dollars an hour and I liked the challenge of working with the men on the docks. What I didn't like was thinking I had to prove anything to Tommy. I didn't, and the memory of my dad's face every time he had to deal with Tommy's bullshit was burned into my mind. The safest bet was to assume Tommy was a loser. That bet usually paid off.

A few days later, however, I did what he said and showed up at the union hall across the street from the port. I expected to find huge guys with bulging forearms like Popeye, but what I found was a mix of black and white, thin and fat, stubborn and sullen. When Tommy showed up, he was the youngest and strongest looking of the lot of them.

Oh, how Tommy could work a room. He clapped me on the back and introduced me to everyone. He had an amazing memory for names and he introduced me to so many people that I forgot, literally, the name of every single one of them. He knew them all.

Then we headed out to the parking lot.

"This is the most important part," Tommy said. "You got to meet Tricky. He's the head of the union and he does the hiring."

At the back of the parking lot was an old champagne-colored Monte Carlo. At the wheel was a thick man with tangled gray hair and a beard. There was a short line of men coming away from his window and we got in it. As guys would lean in to talk to Tricky, they'd shake hands, exchange a few words, and then walked away.

"Tricky!" Tommy said with a big smile. Tricky grinned; he liked Tommy, too. They shook hands. "Hey, this is my brother," Tommy said and patted me on the back. "You think you're going to have enough gangs today?"

"I don't know," Tricky said. Just then, Tommy reached into his pocket and in an instant, he had passed a folded bill to Tricky.

"We'll see you inside," Tricky said and we walked away.

When we were out of earshot, I said, "What was that all about?"

"That's how you make 18 dollars an hour," Tommy said. "We're not in the union, so he's going to take all the union guys, and then he's going to fill out the gangs with non-union people."

"You have to pay him for that?" I asked.

"Yup," Tommy said. "You see all these guys? They want jobs, too. If you want to work, you have to make it worth his while."

I wanted to leave. Tommy was always involved in something shady. Everything he did was on the down-low one way or the other. But, I wasn't going to give him the satisfaction of seeing me run.

Back in the union hall, Tommy handed me a small card with my name on it.

"I filled this out already," he said. "When you see me hold mine up, hold yours up and we'll get in."

A few minutes later, it all went down just like Tommy said it would. Tricky came into the hall and climbed up on a table. He looked strong in an untrained, beat-up kind of way.

As he scanned the room, the other guys crowded around. Tommy and I held back. The longshoreman held up their union cards, and Tricky collected them. His mouth moved as he counted them off. After all the union cards were collected, he looked out at the remaining men.

The black ones were aggressive. They crowded in tighter.

"Right here, boss!" one of them said as he waved his non-union card.

Tricky looked over them. He pointed at a white guy at the back of the room and that guy came forward, handed Tricky his card, and left. It happened again and again. The black ones were getting more agitated. When he picked a black one, the rest crowded in even closer. When his head turned our way, Tommy raised his card and I did as well. Tricky nodded with his eyes, we pushed through, gave him our cards, and headed out the back door. We were hired.

We walked from the back of the union hall, crossed the street, and then down a long pier past the old turn-of-the-century warehouses. A pelican swooped down to the water and scooped up a fish as we headed for the waterfront where the crane towers were. Everyone was quiet except Tommy. He never stopped. No one else was talking unless it was to him. He was positively athletic in his ability to walk and chatter and slap backs at the same time.

The sun was getting higher and hotter when we reached the end of the pier. We were on a long concrete waterfront dotted with forklifts, crates, and two tall cranes. Tied off on the giant pier were several big barges. They were empty and sitting high in the water.

"Is that what we're doing today?" I asked. "Loading these barges?"

"Yup," Tommy said. "Hundred and ten pounds pound sacks of bulgur wheat."

He must have detected my anxiety which I was trying to hide.

"Don't worry," he said. "Just pace yourself, do what you're told, and you'll be alright." He smiled a big, confident smile and clapped me on the back and it worked. I knew I would be OK.

A few minutes later, Tricky came out with a clipboard and assigned everyone to work gangs of four each.

I moved with the crowd of guys I had been assigned to. They seemed to know where they were going, so I just followed. We stepped off the dock and onto one of the rusty barges and then lined up at a ladder. When it was my turn I followed the man in front of me down into the hole.

My eyes adjusted to the dark as I climbed down a ladder that was welded to the inside of the barge. It was big inside; at least 40 feet deep and as wide as it was tall and twice as long. Once everyone was down and quiet, we could hear the water lapping the sides of the barge. I was standing in a giant metal rectangle that was empty and smelled like diesel fuel and dirt.

I followed my gang to one part of the barge and the other four men went to another part. The largest man in my group was a big black dude who was thick and strong-looking. He had a bandana on his head and was pulling on a pair of gardening gloves.

"You ever done this before?" he asked me.

"No," I said.

The other two guys snickered.

"Then you do what the fuck I tell you," he said. "In a minute, they going to start lowering pallets of sacks in here, and we got to spread them out along the walls and then the floors. That's all we do; we spread the sacks out even so this whole motherfucker is full up when we done."

"I can do that," I said.

"We'll see," he said. "What's your name?"

"Josh," I said.

He offered his hand soul style.

"I'm Ricky," he said. "These two bitches here ain't worth knowing."

When we heard the big diesel crane start, everyone stared up at the hatch. Seconds later, a pallet of white sacks hovered overhead and then was lowered down to the floor of the barge. It came to rest right in the center. All eight of us rushed forward. The bars at the end of the thick metal line were pulled out from the lip of the pallet so the line went slack. The crane motor revved up and the line was retracted. The metal bars clanged together as the line disappeared over our heads.

Then, I did what Ricky did. The stack was shoulder high, so Ricky pulled a sack onto his big shoulder and walked to the far corner of the barge. I pulled a sack onto my shoulder and suddenly found out exactly what 110 pounds feels like; it's heavy. I walked it over and dropped it right beside Ricky's bag.

"We line the walls and then work our way back to the middle," he said. "Make one layer, then another. At the end of the day, this whole motherfucker gonna full and we just step out."

When the stack on the pallet was down to waist high, I couldn't heft the bags up to my shoulders anymore. I had to clutch them to my chest. When I dropped a bag into place, the plastic cross stitch on the bag dragged across my forearm. I noticed for the first time that everyone else had on gloves and long sleeves and now I knew why.

Just as the pallet was emptied, another appeared over our heads. It was lowered, and two of the guys pulled the metal bars out, walked them over to the empty pallet, and slid them under the lip. The empty pallet was taken away and we all descended on the full pallet.

On the third pallet, Ricky gave me some tips.

"Keep your back straight," he said. "Don't try to manhandle the bags. That shit will wear you out. Just guide them in place."

He would slide the bags onto his big shoulders and skillfully place them where he wanted them. When the stack was high, he could do two at a time. When the stack was low, he'd flip a bag up to his shoulders before walking. His technique was perfect and he moved gracefully without any wasted motion.

We lined the walls and worked our way to the middle and then we were walking on the bags we had previously placed. This introduced a whole new peril. The bags flexed underfoot, and there were spaces between them. I stepped into one of the spaces and tripped.

"That's why we got to place these motherfuckers tight, right beside each other," Ricky said. "You can break your leg that way."

After a while, everyone fell into a rhythm and we'd have a minute between pallets. I was good when the stack was high and I could slip the heavy sack onto my shoulder. When I had to clean and jerk the bag up to my shoulder or clutch it to my chest, I slowed way down. The other men kept the pace. By lunch, I was exhausted but we were standing on bags that filled up half of the barge.

On the pier, Tommy handed me a ham sandwich and we sat down. He had already eaten off the lunch truck parked at the end of the dock.

"Thanks," I said. I loosened the laces on my shoes.

"Look at your arms," he said. "I should have told you to wear long sleeves."

"Those sacks might as well be made of sandpaper," I said. "Ricky showed me how to guide the bags so they don't drag over your arms but I'm not that good at it."

"Ricky is a bull," Tommy said. "I used to play football against him."

"You guys are the same age?" I asked. Ricky looked to be at least a decade older.

"Yeah," he said. "He's been working down here a long time."

I noticed his speech was a little slow and then saw his eyes were bloodshot and glassy. He was high.

"You're not on a gang?" I asked.

"No way," he said. "I did my time in the hole. I'm on a forklift inside."

I got two Cokes from the lunch truck and drank those down and then went back in the hole.

"You used to play football with Tommy?" I asked Ricky after we got back to work.

"Yeah, I used to play football with that pothead," he said. For some reason, that comment stung me. "How you know him?"

"He's my brother. Half-brother, actually."

"You got the smart half," Ricky said. "Tommy talks all the time but never says nothing. But, that little motherfucker was fast. He was world-class fast. If he was bigger, he would have played college ball."

"What about you?" I asked. "You're big enough."

"I met a bunch of college scouts," Ricky said. "Florida State wanted me. But, I just never filled out the paperwork and no one showed me how. Ain't nobody never looked out for Ricky but Ricky. I started working here and then I moved around… They probably couldn't find me after that. I just never followed through."

At the end of the day, the barge was full of sacks and much lower in the water. We spread the last pallet and climbed out.

Inside the warehouse, I saw Tommy talking to Tricky, but when he saw me, he jumped up and we left. He kept talking all the way to the car and then most of the way home. He was high, but mostly, that was just him. I thanked him when he dropped me off, and he was gracious.

"No problem, brother!" he said. He seemed genuinely happy.

On the second day, Tommy had me pay Tricky in the parking lot. He gave me a $20 and I passed it on to Tricky. I worked with the same gang and the work got easier. This time, I had long sleeves and gloves. Ricky made the time pass by singing and cracking jokes and moving bags faster than anyone else.

At the end of the week, we were loading cornmeal in 50-pound sacks made out of cloth and it was so easy that we had a lot of time to sit down.

The next week, Ricky was in a bad mood and everyone was quiet. We went back to the 110-pound sacks. Everyone was staring up at the opening when the first pallet came into view. Suddenly, the line went slack and the pallet went into a free fall. Then the line straightened out and the pallet jerked to a halt. The sudden stop made the neatly stacked bags rain down. Everyone ran to the sides. The sacks made a loud thud when they hit the metal floor in the empty barge and then it was quiet.

After a moment, the pallet was lowered the rest of the way, but Ricky was furious. He headed up the ladder while the rest of us cleared the pallet and spread out the sacks that had survived the fall.

Ricky returned a few minutes later but didn't say anything. I waited a while before I asked what he found out.

"Motherfucker is high," he said. "Keep clear when them pallets coming down. Jackass will drop them on your head."

We stayed well to the sides when the pallets would lower down. They came down in a jerky uneven motion but none of the bags fell off for the rest of the day. Still, everything took longer. When quitting time came, we stayed in the hole and kept working and finished at sundown.

When we stepped out of the barge, I saw Ricky head into the warehouse. He was pissed. A couple of the other guys noticed and they followed him. "Ricky's going to fuck someone up!" one of them said.

I watched from the giant warehouse door. Ricky walked up to a skinny white dude and pushed him hard. The white dude flew backward and landed on his ass. Several men jumped in front of Ricky.

"You motherfuckers doing drugs in here!" he yelled. "Going to get one of us killed down in the hole!"

Several of the men said something to Ricky, but I couldn't hear them.

"I grew up down here, motherfucker!" Ricky yelled.

There was more talk, and then Tricky arrived. Ricky got nose to nose with Tricky but I couldn't hear what he was saying. Tricky didn't flinch or speak or turn away. He was stone.

Finally, Ricky turned and left.

In the parking lot, I found Tommy asleep in his car. He had waited for me.

We didn't work for a couple of days after that, but Tommy came by for dinner. When my mom left the room, I asked him about what he heard.

"I don't ask a lot of questions," he said.

"Are they dealing drugs?" I asked.

"Hey, I don't know what they do there, but I'll tell you this; if they're moving drugs, Ricky is involved," Tommy said. "I'm on probation, so I don't get involved. Don't ask any questions, make your money, and go home. That's what I do."

Ricky was in a good mood as we worked through the next shifts. The pallets came down, smooth and sure, and we unloaded them quickly and had a lot of time to sit down. It rained through several shifts and while that made the bags slick, it kept us wet and cool.

I noticed that Ricky ate alone at lunchtime. He would go inside the warehouse, sit up high on a ledge, and eat out of a paper sack. Tommy was usually talking to someone while I ate. If he was high, he'd eat more, but most of the time he wasn't. Normally, he was in a good mood and laughing. He always had food waiting for me when I came out of the hole.

A couple of weeks clocked by and it was a Friday and everyone was in a good mood. We were waiting in the empty barge for the first pallet to come down. Pete was a guy in the other gang. He was smoking a cigarette when we heard the crane motor rev up. He looked up and saw the pallet arrive overhead. He dropped his cigarette and crushed it out with his boot.

In my memory, everything that happened next was lightning fast and in slow motion. The pallet came to a sudden halt and a single bag slid off the top. The falling bag clipped Pete right in the back of the head. He toppled forward and for an instant, I saw the top of his spine sticking out of his back at the neckline of his shirt.

For an awful second, no one moved. It was quiet. Then, the loaded pallet started down. Everyone was frozen except Ricky. He grabbed the bag and slung it off Pete's head and then grabbed Pete's hands and dragged him out of the way. The pallet landed in a pool of blood.

Suddenly, there was a lot of yelling. Ricky didn't move away from Pete's body but several other men went up the ladder. A few minutes later, Tommy yelled down at me and asked if I was OK. I gave him a sickly thumbs up. Tricky looked in and then was gone. Ricky and I and a few others emptied the pallet and then Ricky dragged Pete to the pallet and laid him gently on it. Pete's face and hands were stark white. Blood was everywhere. His head flopped back and forth and then the pallet took him away. When I followed Ricky up the ladder, I saw Tricky was waiting for us.

"All of you go home," he said to everyone standing there. To Ricky, he said, "Come with me."

"Where is that motherfucker?" Ricky asked. His voice was low and full of fury.

"He's already gone," Tricky say.

When I got back to the car, Tommy was waiting for me.

"Crazy day," he said.

"Was the crane driver high?" I asked.

"I don't know," Tommy said.

"Bullshit!" I said. I was in no mood for it. "You know everything. You're high half the time, too. Was he high?"

"You don't have to work here if it's too much for you," he said. "Crazy shit happens down here."

"What's going to happen next?" I asked.

"Ricky will have to deal with Tricky if he tries anything," Tommy said. "They don't get along at all. That's why Ricky's still in the hole."

"I think all you guys up the warehouse are moving drugs and getting high," I said.

"Maybe you best not go back if that's how you feel," he said.

"Oh, I'm going back," I said. "You think you're tougher than me, but you're not. I want the money. But the crane operator got a man killed today. I hope Ricky finds that guy and fucks him up."

I couldn't believe what I was saying. It didn't sound like me. I had been afraid of Tommy. Now, suddenly, I wasn't.

For a couple of days, Tricky wasn't there. They put up a sign at the union hall that read 'Union Only.' I called Tommy to tell him not to come to work.

On the third day, the 'Union Only' sign was still up so I went home. My mom made me breakfast and then stood in the kitchen reading the newspaper.

"This town is getting worse and worse," she said. "Did you know this guy? It says here he worked at the port."

She read aloud from the paper.

"The body of a man who washed up on Sanders Beach has been identified as 48-year-old Gerald Simms, a long-time port employee," she read. "Blah blah blah... Police are awaiting toxicology reports to determine if Mr. Simms was under the influence of any substances when he drowned and are also seeking to determine how long he had been in the water. Mr. Simms was a long-time port employee who held a variety of positions in his 29 years there, including warehouse supervisor and crane operator."

She looked up at me and must have detected a look in my eyes.

"You knew him?" she asked.

I snapped out of it and went into cover mode.

"No," I said. "There are a lot of people who work there. I never heard of him."

I called Tommy but there was no answer. When I called again in the afternoon, he picked up.

"Yeah, I heard about it," he said. "The guy drowned. That's what the paper said."

"Was it the same guy?" I asked.

"The same guy what?"

"The same guy that was on the crane when Pete was killed!" I said, exasperated.

"Yeah, it was him. So, what?" Now I could tell he was high. "He was a good guy, but he didn't listen. Tricky warned him lots of times, but he was a senior person in the union. Tricky couldn't fire him."

"Warned him about what?" I asked.

There was a long pause and then I heard Tommy exhale.

"Warned him about getting high at work," he said. "But he didn't have to listen. He was the senior person in the union."

That night, Tommy called back. He wasn't high anymore.

"Tomorrow, they'll be hiring," he said. "Don't, as in do not, talk to anyone about anything. I'm serious as a heart attack, dude. We're just there for the money and these union guys are stone-cold killers. So don't go running your mouth. Got it? I'm serious."

I didn't like being told what to do by Tommy, but I understood exactly what he was telling me.

"I got it," I said. "I won't say anything."

"Don't make me sorry I got you on down there," he continued, "because if anything happens to you, Dad will blame me and he hates me already. You're his favorite. You always have been."

"I'll keep my mouth shut, I promise," I said and we both said good night, but I couldn't get the last thing he said out of my mind. We both knew it was true and now it had been said out loud.

The next morning, when I handed Tricky the money in the parking lot, he stared me down hard. He looked right into my eyes, but I gave him nothing, and he hired us both.

Ricky was down in the hole when I got there. I smiled and we shook hands but he didn't say much all day. There was a silence when he heard the crane motor start. Everyone stayed well clear of the center of the barge. No one said anything about Pete.

The summer wore on and it got really hot down in the hole. Everyone was quiet and moved slowly. We had to take breaks where we got out of the barge and went into the warehouse to cool off. We'd get 10 minutes out of every 90 to cool down.

Tricky had an office in the warehouse made from a gardening shed and it had a window AC unit. There were always union guys in Tricky's office laughing or watching TV, but Ricky stayed with us. We were all soaked with sweat by the second break period, and Ricky made sure the 10 minutes would stretch out to 20 in the afternoon.

"How long have you been in the union?" I asked him one day when no one else was around. He was drinking a coke and looking at all the guys packed into Tricky's office.

"You mean why ain't I in there with those motherfuckers?" he said, gesturing with his coke can at the office.

"Well, yeah," I said.

"I used to move a lot of weed outta here for them," he said. "The crews on the different boats would bring it in from Mexico, and then I'd take a lot of it back out to my neighborhood. But then I stopped, and no one likes an ex-pusher."

"Why did you stop?" I asked.

"Too dangerous," he said. "People get shot. People go to jail, then get shot later. Plus, I didn't want to make them any richer. They look like a bunch of redneck motherfuckers, but they got money somewhere. They been moving drugs out of this place for a long time and never been caught. Tricky's smart; he don't leave no traces."

"But…" I said. I wanted to ask more.

He looked over at me and then started laughing.

"What the fuck you doing down here, man?" he asked. "Just 'cause you related to Tommy, that don't mean you got any business down here mixed up with this shit."

"I'm just here for the money like everybody else," I said.

"Niggar, please. You're a fucking tourist. You'll go off to college one day," he said. "But don't you worry about Ricky. I been taking care of myself for a long time."

He walked out of the warehouse but a second later, he stuck his head back in.

"But maybe you shouldn't stand too close to me down in the hole," he said, his face somber.

I nodded soberly, but then he busted out laughing again and walked away.

The following Monday, Ricky didn't show for work. The other guys all looked somber, and after a few minutes, before the first pallet was lowered, I asked, to no one in particular, "Where's Ricky?"

No one answered. Everyone just stared at me like I had said something really stupid or looked away.

On our first break, I found Tommy on a forklift and climbed up to the seat. I leaned in close so he could hear me over the forklift motor.

"Where's Ricky?" I asked.

Tommy looked at me, stricken, and then he flashed a fake smile and started nodding.

"Yeah, man, cool! I'll talk to you at lunch," he said.

I knew then that Ricky was dead. At lunch, I avoided Tommy, ate, and then went back down in the hole. I didn't look at anyone and no one looked at me.

That night, Tommy came by the house. I heard him speak to my mom when he entered, and after a minute, he entered my bedroom and sat down on the bed.

"You aren't working down there anymore," he said. "It's just too hot right now."

"What happened to Ricky?" I asked.

"He got shot up in his neighborhood," he said. "People in his neighborhood get shot all the time."

"People who deal drugs," I said.

"Yeah, people who deal drugs, people in the wrong place at the wrong time," he said.

"Ricky didn't do drugs and he didn't deal drugs," I said.

"What, you think you know him?" Tommy asked. "That guy was a hard-core dealer and a killer himself. He was union, he moved a lot of drugs, and he got shot. That's what happened."

"Why can't I go back?" I asked.

"Because it's too hot," he said. "I don't want to have to look out for you or tell any lies. I'm not good at it."

"What kind of lies would you have to tell?" I asked.

"Like telling Tricky that you don't know anything about Ricky, that you guys didn't ever talk," he said. He was getting agitated and his voice was rising. "I know it's good money, but you can't come back. You can't."

I felt sorry for Tommy suddenly. He was small in more ways than I could count.

"Why are you there?" I asked. "You've had other jobs. Are you dealing for them?"

"What do you care if I am?" he said. He was angry now. "You sit here in mommy and daddy's house judging what people do. Maybe you don't remember, but I spent three years and eight months in prison and I'm not going back. I'm not dealing drugs for them. I just work there."

He took a deep breath and we sat there in silence for a long, painful moment.

"I'm pushing 30 and no one is going to take care of me anymore. I'm close to getting into the union and then I can work full time with benefits. I don't want you to fuck that up for me, so just stay away," he said. "Tricky might not hire you anyway, but I'm asking, for me, just stay away, OK?"

I would have stayed away for him. While I didn't love him like a brother, I knew he wanted love from me, if only as a way to get love from my dad second-hand.

A few days later, a police detective knocked on our door. My mom answered. When she entered my room, I saw a fearful look on her face. The detective asked a few basic questions while she listened, then he asked that I meet him at the police station and answer more questions.

"What do you want to talk to him about?" she said to the detective as he was walking out the door. "What's going on?"

"We're looking into a shooting that happened in Brownsville that we think is related to activities at the port," he said. "The victim was an African-American named Richard Jeffries."

My mother put her hand over her mouth and looked at me.

"Did you know him?" she asked.

"Yes," I said. "He was on my gang."

"Your gang?" she whispered.

"It's just a term for a crew that works inside the ships," I said. "It doesn't mean what you think."

"You know how to get to the police station downtown, don't you?" the detective asked me.

When the detective left, my mom was pale and woozy with fear.

"You don't know anything about this, do you?" she asked.

The lie tumbled forth without a problem.

"No," I said. "We never talked or anything. I was the low man on the totem pole. No one talks to me."

She called my dad and put him on the phone.

"This somehow involves Tommy and drugs, doesn't it?" he asked.

Next lie queued up.

"No," I said. "All I did was load ships. I don't know anything. Neither does Tommy."

As my dad asked more questions, I covered up more. Up until then, I had been very close to my parents and never felt as if there was anything I couldn't discuss with them. But now, I didn't want them to know about my life. I had seen a man have his head nearly ripped off. I knew about two probable murders, and I just didn't want to talk to them anymore. It was my life now.

"I'll meet you there," my dad said.

"No way," I said, trying not to sound panicked. The last thing I wanted was my dad present for what I suspected was coming. "I can answer questions on my own, and since I don't know anything, I'll be in and out of there fast. I do not want you there."

"You need to have a lawyer present," he said.

We went back and forth like this for a while and then I handed the phone back to my mom and took a shower. Things were coming into focus in my mind quickly. I realized I had taken the job at the port to prove something to Tommy. He had always positioned himself as tougher, as more streetwise than me, and he treated me like I was somehow weak because I had married parents who loved me. He looked down on me as being sheltered and weak. Now, he and I were in some deep shit together, and I was not about to involve my parents. No lawyer, no mom, and dad, no help.

On the way in to the police station, I walked past a squad car and saw Tricky sitting in the back. His hands were cuffed. He looked at me and we locked eyes. His eyes were burning with cold fury.

The detective was distracted and perfunctory. When he started to ask questions, he didn't look up from his notepad. He asked how I knew Ricky, and if I had ever seen Ricky deal drugs. He asked if I had ever seen Ricky high. He asked who Ricky was close to at the port. As he continued, I could see that I wasn't going to have to lie to the police. I had never seen Ricky do drugs or deal drugs, and Ricky didn't hang out with anyone. The detective asked nothing about Pete, the crane driver, the union, or Tricky.

When the detective was finished, I asked "Was Ricky dealing drugs?"

"He had that history," the detective said, "and once people get into that life, they rarely leave it. Eventually, they get shot."

I left the police station and a few minutes later, saw Tommy in the car behind me. I pulled over at a gas station and he came up to my window. He was breathing heavily with panic.

"Holy shit, man! What did you do?" he asked.

"I didn't do anything," I said. I told Tommy how the detective had just shown up at the house, how I had gone down to the station to talk, and how the police hadn't asked me anything important, but my story didn't calm him. He was sweating with fear.

"They arrested Tricky for possession and he thinks they're looking for a way to connect him to Ricky," Tommy said, "and now he knows you went to the police!"

"I didn't go to the police; the police came to me!" I said. "And you tell Tricky that while I was prepared to lie, I didn't have to because they didn't ask me anything important. They just asked me what I knew about Ricky, and I told them not much."

"You don't understand, man!" he said. "These guys will kill you. They'll kill Dad to get to you!"

For some reason, looking back, I wasn't scared. I was sorry for Tommy, I was sorry that all his potential and talent had come to this, but I wasn't scared.

"They aren't going to kill Dad," I said. "And they aren't going to do shit to me, because if there's one thing I learned down there, it's that those guys murder their own. I was just a tourist. You're the one that wants into their shit union. So, watch your own back, brother."

With that, I started my car and drove away. I saw him in my rear-view mirror literally pulling his hair in frustration and fear.

That night, my dad asked a lot of questions. I told him that I knew they moved drugs through the port, but I didn't know how much, what kind, or who did what.

"Is Tommy involved?" my dad asked.

"I don't think so," I said. "He does drugs, but I don't think he deals them."

My dad looked down. That answer seemed to both satisfy him and confirm his suspicions.

"Don't talk to anyone about it," he said. "And stay away from your brother."

He got up and went to the kitchen. I heard the tinkling of ice in a highball glass.

Two days later, I came home from a job interview and saw my dad slumped over on a lawn chair in the backyard. If he was home in the middle of the day, something was wrong. He had an empty highball glass in his hand. My mom came out of the kitchen and her eyes were bloodshot from crying.

"Tommy was killed in a forklift accident," she said.

What followed was an acid trip of details, tears, trips to the hospital, a long meeting at a funeral home where my dad wept and wept, and a night-long vigil with my mom at the kitchen table. She told me some details about how she and my dad met and how my dad's first wife had tried to undermine their relationship by poisoning Tommy's impression of her. He was thrown into the middle of that chaotic period and when I was born, he wanted nothing to do with me because I was taking his dad away from him. I didn't tell her that he had essentially confirmed those feelings to me.

Tommy was buried next to his mother a few days later. Dara arrived, and she was stricken to silence. She barely looked at me. A few of his high school friends were there, but that was it. It was over quickly.

The police never came around to ask any questions. His death was classified as an accident. He had no assets to distribute.

I got a job in a popular nightclub and worked as a doorman for a short period before they moved me behind the bar. People showed me their ID and no one gave me any shit. Something had turned over in me and now I projected a certain menace.

There was a lot of partying during this period, but I saved money and eventually was ready to go away to college. My dad advised me to study pharmacology and that was a good move. I was good at chemistry, I discovered.

For a while, I dated a girl that was a film student and she took me to see "On The Waterfront" with Marlon Brando. In the opening scene, a man is pushed off a building for talking to the police about corruption on the waterfront. The corrupt union enforced the unspoken rules and chose who got the plum jobs. When the famous scene with Brando and his older brother came on the screen, I couldn't move. I started breathing hard and left the theater.

Later, I rented a copy and watched it by myself. "I was your kid brother," Brando said to Rod Steiger. "You should have looked out for me."

That scene made me lower my head and weep for the first time about what had happened. Tommy did look out for me, I thought. Maybe I should have looked out for him. I was the smarter one. I was the one that was loved. I was the one that was from a home with a mother and father that loved each other and doted on me. My mom wasn't crazy. I had no little brother who I feared was my dad's favorite. I was the more mature brother, the emotionally undamaged one, and I should have looked out for him. Instead, I last saw him in my rearview mirror, alone and afraid.

After college, I took a job in a pharmacy. Six months later, I was a salesman for a pharmaceutical company. I had a car allowance and a cell phone and was on the road a lot. I made a lot of money and dated a lot of girls. At one point, I was sleeping with three different women, and it was crazy. My cell phone rang all the time.

One day it rang, and I saw it was my mother. She rarely called me.

"Hi, Mom!" I said. I was in my car and looked forward to killing some time catching up with her. But it wasn't to be. She called to tell me that my dad had been killed in a car wreck. He was drunk and he ran off the road and hit a pine tree. No one else was injured and he had died instantly.

She was not the same after that. Her whole life was tied up with my dad. They were deeply in love. A few weeks later, she moved in with her sister in Texas and I knew I wouldn't see her much.

Everyone was gone now, and I was on my own.

After a few years, I went to work for a company that made insulin. The number of diabetics in the country was on the rise, so insulin was a growth market. It was an easy sell since my company was the top insulin manufacturer and doctors prescribed it in volume. I wasn't repping anything groundbreaking, so the meetings were mostly social. I took a lot of people out to dinner, and it was easy money.

I was dropping off lunch for my top prescribing doctor when I saw an older man who used a walker coming down the hallway. I had no trouble recognizing Tricky. I put my bags down and found a way to turn my back on him. When he stopped at the reception desk, I looked over at him. His hair was dirty as were his clothes. I listened as the receptionist booked his next appointment. That's how I learned his real name; Michael Deakins.

After he left, I said to the receptionist, "I don't recall meeting with that patient. Is he new?"

"Oh, he's Medicaid," she said. "He's had all kinds of problems, and he comes in a lot because we give him free samples and supplies."

As I unpacked the lunch, I looked at her pad and saw his record. Under his name was his address. Now, I knew Tricky's real name, his address, I knew he was poor, and I knew he was weak and vulnerable. Those were not good things for me to know.

That night, I looked on Google maps and saw he lived in a trailer way out in the country. He had no neighbors. Now, I also knew he was isolated.

For a while, I just thought about what I might do. Tommy had been dead for over a decade. Tricky was old and in poor health and would die soon. Still, I wanted him to see me succeeding in life while he was now a miserable, poor, dying wretch. The tables had turned; it was he that was weak and vulnerable, and me that had the power.

One day, Dara called. We rarely spoke after Tommy's death, and I always felt she blamed me in some way. She was calling to report on our mom. Our mother was suffering from some sort of "emotional illness," as Dara called it. She was describing depression, but I didn't say anything. She asked if I could call more often, and I said I would.

After that call, I knew I was going to move away. Whatever I was going to do, if I was going to do it, I needed to do it now.

I drove down the highway to Tricky's home and confirmed he lived in a ramshackle trailer. The trailer was well off the road on former farm property. A single pole that took one thin electrical line to the trailer and a mailbox was at the road, but the trailer was at least 100 yards from any passing traffic.

There was no doubt he lived there; his same old Monte Carlo was parked beside the trailer. It had flat tires and faded paint, but it was the car he was in when we paid him off for a job. I drove by again at night and saw the lights on. He was in there.

I came to my plan one night after getting an email from Dara. Mom was worse than ever. She missed my dad, Dara wrote, and wasn't moving on from his death. Dara was thinking of moving her to a psychiatric facility. The time had come for me to move closer to her which meant Tricky was going to die. It was that simple.

A week later, I manufactured a reason to stop by Tricky's doctor's office so I could look up his medical record. The girls that ran the office were computer illiterates so they didn't realize what I could access. In his record, I saw he was a double amputee. His feet had developed gangrene so they were removed and he had prosthetics. His prescription was for long-acting insulin called Lantus, but as I had hoped, he also took fast-acting insulin called Humalog. Too much Humalog and Tricky's blood glucose levels would crash. Without intervention, he would blackout, and then, he would die.

I left my house late that afternoon. Near Tricky's house was a fire access road lined by a tall stand of pine trees. I eased my car slowly down the fire road and parked out of sight and quietly waited for darkness.

When I could see stars overhead, I walked to his trailer. As I came to the door, I could hear his TV. I knocked. Nothing. I knocked louder. The TV was turned down.

"Who is it?" he said. He was irritated.

"This is Bob Jones from the Lantus Corporation, Mr. Deakins," I said. "I understand you're running low on supplies, so I brought some out to you."

He took a while to get to the door, but finally, it cracked open and I saw him standing there on his fake feet. He looked right at me in the light that spilled out the door.

"Hi," I said. "I have some samples and a couple of things to show you. May I come in?"

He was suspicious.

"No one ever comes to my house for this," he said.

I pulled out one of his doctor's business cards and handed it to him.

"Your doctor sent me here," I said. "Your doctor said you have trouble getting your medications, and our company has a program to provide samples and supplies to people who are struggling. It's strictly a courtesy and you're under no obligation."

He looked at the doctor's card, and then opened the door and turned away. He hadn't recognized me. I stepped in, shut the door, and locked it.

I had decided that I wasn't going to maintain the ruse once I was inside. He was still a big man, and he had survived a lot, and he was a killer. I was going to do what I was going to do and get out.

Before he had even turned around, I grabbed him by the collar and yanked him backward. I swept my leg under his feet and he landed flat on his back. I rolled him over on his stomach before he could recover, drilled my knee into his back, and pulled out a set of handcuffs. I grabbed one of his hands, and he resisted, but he was very weak so I was able to pull both hands together and cuff him.

I rolled him on his back and put a knee on his chest. I let my full weight come to bear and lowered my face to his.

"Time to pay the piper, Tricky," I said.

"What the fuck," he said, gasping.

When I got up and went to his kitchen, he said, "This is bullshit. I'm retired. I don't owe nothing."

"Oh, I think you do," I said as a looked in his refrigerator. In the door were several vials of Humalog and very little food.

I came back and stood where he could see me. His eyes were darting around. I took a 100cc syringe out of my pocket and that caught his attention. I needed a large syringe to deliver a fatal dose of the Humalog.

"You don't recognize me?" I asked. He watched me draw the clear Humalog into the big syringe. "Do you remember Ricky?"

"I don't know no fucking Ricky, man. I'm retired and I paid my dues," he said. He tried to push himself with his fake feet, but one of them had popped out of place when he fell.

"No? How about Tommy," I asked. "Do you remember him?"

He was starting to put it all together.

"I don't know a Tommy, man," he said, but he was less convincing. "Who are you?"

I kneeled beside him and held the big needle up so he could see it.

"You remember Tommy. He wanted to be in your union really bad," I said. I yanked his shirt up exposing his fat belly.

Tricky was quiet for a minute, then he gave up pretending.

"You're that little brother," he said.

"That's right, I'm that little brother," I said, "and I had a big brother. What happened to him?"

"He got run over. It was an accident," Tricky said.

"What happened to Ricky?" I asked.

"He got shot. No one knows who did it," he said.

"Someone knows," I said. "And I think that someone is you."

"You don't know shit. You were a little panty waste and so was your fucking brother," he said. I was seeing the old Tricky now, behind the gray hair and the old age bloat and the big nose. He was in there.

"In a second," I said, "I'm going to inject this fast-acting insulin in you, and then, in about 10 minutes, your blood sugar is going to drop. You're going to go lower and lower, and then you're going to black out. And sometime after that, your brain is going to stop telling your heart to beat, and you're going to be dead. No one is going to know what happened, and I doubt anyone is going to care."

I told him all of this slowly and deliberately. His face was a stone.

"So, this is your last chance," I continued. "In your miserable life, I'm the last person you'll ever talk to. This is the end, Tricky. So tell me; why did you kill Tommy?"

He laughed.

"I don't remember. I killed a lot of people," he said.

"That's it? You don't remember?" I said.

He smiled and I could see his yellow teeth and smell his rancid breath.

"He was a loser," Tricky said. "He was always talking. Drove everyone crazy. No one trusted him. We didn't want to let him in the union and we didn't want to let him go because he knew too much."

"You're making this a lot easier," I said. "Get ready to burn in hell."

Down around his waistline, just below the navel, I drove the needle in deep, hoping to avoid as much of his belly fat as possible. He flinched, cried out, and wriggled around, but I depressed the plunger and yanked the needle out. All of the insulin was delivered. I took a couch cushion and put it over his face so I didn't have to look at him.

I stood up and found his smaller needles and drew some Humalog into one, squirted it out on the floor, and then dropped the needle beside him. I wiped down the Humalog vial and put it back in the refrigerator and wiped down everything I had touched in the kitchen. During this time, he didn't move.

After I staged and cleaned everything, I sat down and watched TV. I glanced down at him, but couldn't see his face. He wasn't moving. The commercial breaks came and went.

After a few minutes, I lift the cushion off his face. His eyes were closed and his breathing was shallow and labored. I took a glucose monitor out of my pocket and used the pen to prick his finger. He didn't flinch. I wicked a blood spec onto the test strip and the monitor gave a reading. He was at 20. He was clammy and sweating because he was dying. His blood glucose level was headed to zero and his brain was about to run out of gas. He'd die shortly after.

I rolled him over enough to get the cuffs off him and left quickly, closing the door behind me. There were no cars on the road. No one had seen a thing.

The days clocked by and everything was fine. Dara called and told me my mom was the same, maybe a little better.

After two weeks, I drove by Tricky's trailer. Nothing had changed. The old Monte Carlo was still there. If he was still inside, he was so decomposed that no one would be able to tell how he died. And, I knew, no one would care.

After Christmas, I decided to move to Houston to be near my mom. I gave my two-week notice and visited my dad's gravesite and then walked over to where Tommy was buried next to his mother. I sat on the grass by his headstone for a while. It was unlikely that I was ever coming back.

On my way out of town, I drove past where Tricky's ramshackle trailer had been, but it was gone. The field where it sat had been recently mowed. Maybe they'll start using it to grow things again, I thought.

My mother improved after I arrived. I started dating again and she liked my new girlfriend. She told me it was time to marry and she was right. My wife and I bought a huge house and later my mom moved in with us. When her grandson was born, she insisted his middle name be Thomas, after my brother, of course. She had always been a better person than Tommy or I.

Death hadn't sainted Tommy, but it made us love and long for him. Death is kind that way.

THE NEW BARBARIANS

When the fall came and the weather changed, he simply bought his own house. He met with the realtor and said "I have a hundred thousand in cash and I make over a hundred thousand a year, and I need a house that fits that budget." Her eyebrows lifted; she knew he was not just shopping. Here was a buyer.

He looked at house after house and after a short time could easily walk into a place and know if it was even possible for him to live there. Some were full of home improvement disasters, and some were near places he didn't want to drive past on his way home. He could see the house as it would look after he moved in. Nick had developed his own sense of style and had the beginnings of an art collection.

At first, he knew vaguely what he wanted, and then as he looked more, he knew exactly what he wanted. When he found something close enough, he directed a short negotiation that broke his way and that was that.

He invited his second wife to see the house before the closing, but they were divorcing, so she didn't have much say so. He needed her present at closing, but other than that, it was to be his house. He had planned to involve her in his decisions or make it look that way and keep her close for as long as it took to bond their child to him. So far, so good; she was participating.

Their child was a happy, big boy and he grew and developed under the wary eye of his older, thinner half-brother. That boy had bounced back and forth between his mother's house, his grandparent's house where his dad was living until they had moved to his dad's new wife's house where he lived with his stepmom and half-brother for half the time, then back to his mom for half the time.

Then there were the new troubles. Now, he would never live with his little brother for any fixed length of time but his dad would have a new house away from his soon-to-be ex-stepmother. The boy adjusted. His dad was fun especially when it was just the two of them. They were constantly on the move. In a sense, the boy was his new Bill.

The first order of business at the house had been to strip out the old kitchen. Nick knew enough about himself to know that if he didn't put in a new kitchen before he moved in, he wouldn't do it at all. He'd make do as he had so many times before. So, he took a few days off work and wrote down a punch list of things that had to get done and started on them.

He turned off the water to the sink and then disconnected all the plumbing. The traps were full of a nasty sludge, but he had the garbage can beside him so everything could be dumped quickly.

Then he used a crowbar and a mallet to detach the countertops from the cabinet bases. He carried them to the driveway and dropped them on a growing pile of debris. Then he removed the cabinets themselves. They unscrewed from the wall but had to be wrestled from the floor.

Behind the cabinets, he discovered huge holes in the sheetrock that had never been repaired. The original contractor had put the cabinets over the holes, and those holes had been letting bugs and rodents in for decades. He could see the droppings built up on the floor beneath the holes. The holes would have to be patched before the new cabinets went in.

He brought the boys by in the afternoons and they played with the hose in the backyard. The older one indulged the younger one now and again but mostly kept to himself. Nick watched them from the bare kitchen. What went on in the older one's head, he wasn't sure, but he knew the boy was sound and healthy. All the signs were there. If Nick didn't have to send such huge checks to their moms every month, he might have a house on the beach, and they would be playing in the surf instead of with a garden hose, but he wouldn't do it differently if that meant the little men in the back yard would not be in the world.

Nick spent more time with Bill. Bill had never had children. He barely dated for a long time and then gave it up for good. Bill had a lot of hobbies and he was both good at and happy with them. Bill had mercifully kept quiet when Nicky announced that his girlfriend was pregnant and he was getting married again. After Nick had tried to explain how it was all a good thing, Bill finally said "Well, you've always had the pink eye of the tiger when it came to the ladies." Bill had nothing to say about the divorce either.

Nick ordered the cabinets for the kitchen from a cabinet maker that was doing a larger job on a bigger house. He had the maker add his cabinet order to the bigger batch which made them a lot cheaper. They were custom, but the bigger house was spreading the costs for him. He didn't patch the holes in the sheetrock until the electrician had come and wired everything in the kitchen for the lighting that would allow him to light the kitchen like a theater stage. All the lights were on dimmers and there were lights over and under the cabinets, inside the boxes, and tiny bar lights hung down over the work areas.

After he patched the sheetrock, he had a plumber come in and re-solder all the pipes with new copper ends and solid handles that would turn the water to the sink on and off. When the cabinets were delivered, he watched as the cabinet maker's guys installed the uppers. He made sure they followed the markings he had made on the sheetrock so they wouldn't cover any of the places the electrician had run new wire.

The tops had to be just so. Nick went to several warehouses looking for the right batch of granite. He needed a lot, and he was ready to pay. Tops were not the place to save money. After agonizing over different shades of Uba-tuba, he settled on a pitch-black set with long emerald green streaks. It was perfect. The bar lights would reflect in the green speckles and give the room a sophisticated, restaurant look. The day they were installed, he let the installers in and left. He hired the most expensive installer and let the guys work. When he came home, he was very pleased. No woman he knew could have done a better job. The kitchen was stunning.

At work, the clients came and went. Orders started and ended. Nick was always near the top of the sales leaderboard. He had the biggest clients and the prestige accounts. He worked them constantly. If the company tried to move an account, the buyer would protest and insist on staying with Nick. He was a steady, sharp performer. Most of the buyers were women.

What was also steady was the complaining about the tone of his emails, which were often sharp like a thrown elbow. Nick was aggressive and when the staffers made a mistake with his client orders, or were late, or forgot, he let them have it.

"You just took a little more money out of my paycheck," he would write. *"Why does this keep happening???"*

The sales manager was an older woman who didn't let anyone finish a sentence and made decisions without gathering many facts. Her emails were short and usually demands that this or that be sold immediately. He didn't respect her or her style, but she didn't know. She was marginally competent, but she liked Nick. He made his numbers.

He knew he was the best salesperson in the office. On the way home, he would shake his head back and forth and smile. Of all the things to be good at, he would be good at the thing that few respected. It was like being the greatest sewer technician. But he was accumulating wealth, and if he did nothing but what he was doing, he would be a millionaire in a few short years.

His job, he knew, was stupid easy, really, and he quietly marveled at how much they paid him for what was so little work. And while he was good at it, he wasn't proud of it. When he worked for a movie studio, he was proud of his little contribution to the whole. Now, he had real responsibility and big clients, but the pride he took in the job was for him.

There were many lessons he had learned in Hollywood in his years there. He learned that some people mean it in the workplace but most don't. Most of the people he worked with didn't mean it. They were all too far away from any center of power. They just had a job, but they didn't care.

Nicky meant it, he cared, but it was all internal. He did his job well for the money and himself. His job was just a coping mechanism that had gone on for a long time and made him relatively wealthy. Resolving his work life was the next great frontier and in his bones, he knew it. He wanted to love it again. Since he had figured out that he would never have a healthy relationship with a woman and ceased to have any faith in that future, work was his new woman, and he wanted it to work.

The boys came and went. They loved his house and him. Nick let them do pretty much what they wanted. They would often just lay on him while he watched his fights on TV. Nick loved MMA. Fighting in a cage made sense, and it had a clear outcome. He and the boys watched fights, went out to eat, and on the weekends, never bathed. They laughed a lot. The boys brought Nick something he had rarely known; actual joy.

The older boy picked up a new attitude towards the black kids at his school. Nick had diligently avoided the subject of race and the boy had made and moved through many friends of both races and there had not been a problem.

At the boy's middle school, the black kids made up a majority, and they flexed their majority muscles. Nick was surprised to get reports from the boy on the aggressiveness of the black females. They were the bullies. Efforts to correct wrongs done to the boy were met with a process that delivered nothing. Nick sent a lot of angry emails to the boy's teachers. He knew the boy was safe but the petty indignities infuriated him.

He and the boy were eating chicken strips in a sports bar when the boy told him another story about what the black girls in his middle school were up to. He asked about the black boys, if they were trouble, and the boy said "They don't do much of anything."

Nick thought about that for a minute. The young black boys at his school had been aggressive and loud and dangerous and he was scared of them. Now, they, too, were passive.

"Well, women are the new men," he said. The boy laughed. His dad was always saying stuff like that. Nicky continued. "Women are the new men and men are the new children."

"What about the children?" the boy asked.

"They're screwed," Nicky said and smiled. "But not you, kid. You're solid gold."

He made minor adjustments and improvements to the house as the years wore on. All the art on the walls gave the place a sophisticated, completed look. Granite countertops and new cabinetry went in all the bathrooms, tile, and wood on all the floors... It was the best house he had ever lived in. Nick had made a house a woman would like, but he had done it on his own.

At night, he drank beer, looked up at the stars, and thought. It was all done now. A great chasm had been crossed. Nicky knew where he was. He had found himself on the map of his own life. Finally, real adulthood was achieved, and it had been done without a woman.

A few girls came and went. He was vulnerable to any women who might chance along, and he knew he always would be. The ones he dated were older and less attractive than the dimes he used to date.

The younger, more attractive women he knew at the office were confident and they supported each other. They acted ruthlessly when they had the power to do so but, of course, any suggestion that they had emerged as self-interested rent-seekers in a world created by men would be vigorously denied, so he never said it.

Nick kept his mouth shut and calculated each interaction with any sexually desirable female like a lion tamer. Any of them could easily reach out and harm him.

He knew his place in his culture and nation as well, and he thought about it often. The country was growing less competent. Imbeciles were in high places. It was easy to see but more and more people succumbed to the corruption. The antiseptic progress around him masked the deeper return to blood, and he knew it. The country wasn't becoming a pluralistic paradise; it was turning on its former leadership class. A great bitterness was sweeping across the land. The future was not bright. Nick looked at his boys and thought about what the white male might have in store in a few short decades.

But then, everything was unlikely. Nicky marveled at his good fortune. A half-century in, he wasn't afraid anymore. If a darker age was to come, he would carry on intact. No one could tell him what to do and he knew what he knew about himself, and his people. He had finally made a separate peace. He had made it alone, and he would pass it on to the boys in time. He owed nothing and looked to nothing and sought nothing except what was good for him. It had not started that way, but this is where it had arrived. And he was OK with it all.

Nada y nada y pues nada.